# My Big, Huge Mistake

M.E. Clayton

Copyright © 2018 Monica Clayton

All rights reserved.

ISBN: 9780463594773

# DEDICATION

For Gene & Linda Oliveira-
   Two people who have blindly and enthusiastically supported everything I've done. Thank you, so, so much! You have no idea how wonderful it feels to be supported so completely!

# CONTENTS

| | |
|---|---|
| Acknowledgments | i |
| Prologue | Pg #1 |
| Chapter 1 | Pg #3 |
| Chapter 2 | Pg #9 |
| Chapter 3 | Pg #13 |
| Chapter 4 | Pg #19 |
| Chapter 5 | Pg #25 |
| Chapter 6 | Pg #31 |
| Chapter 7 | Pg #37 |
| Chapter 8 | Pg #43 |
| Chapter 9 | Pg #49 |
| Chapter 10 | Pg #55 |
| Chapter 11 | Pg #61 |
| Chapter 12 | Pg #67 |
| Chapter 13 | Pg #73 |
| Chapter 14 | Pg #79 |
| Chapter 15 | Pg #85 |
| Chapter 16 | Pg #91 |
| Chapter 17 | Pg #97 |
| Chapter 18 | Pg #103 |
| Chapter 19 | Pg #109 |
| Chapter 20 | Pg #115 |

| | |
|---|---|
| Chapter 21 | Pg #121 |
| Chapter 22 | Pg #127 |
| Chapter 23 | Pg #133 |
| Chapter 24 | Pg #139 |
| Epilogue | Pg #145 |
| Playlist | Pg #147 |
| About the Author | Pg #148 |
| Other Books | Pg #149 |

# ACKNOWLEDGMENTS

The first acknowledgement will always be my husband (unless we ever divorce, then probably not so much after that), but seeing as how I can't imagine that day ever coming, I can't ever put myself out there without thanking him for all his love, support and belief in me.

Second, there's my family; my daughter, my son, my grandchildren, my sister and my mother. They are the people who love me the most, and know me the best and love me dearly, despite, of all they know…LOL!

And, of course, there's my awesome beta, Kamala. She insists that I don't have to thank her in every book, but my love for her and gratitude for all her support and enthusiasm, claims otherwise. She's the first person (outside my family) that I shared this dream with, and she's been by my side every step of the way. Kam, you really are the best kind of friend!

And, finally, I'd like to thank everyone who's purchased, read, reviewed, shared and supported me and my writing. Thank you so much for helping make this dream a reality and a happy, fun one at that! There are not enough 'Thank You's in the world….

# PROLOGUE

Most people claim to be looking at the bride during a wedding. I mean, how could you not? She's supposed to be the attraction to beat all attractions.

This is her day, right?

Well, as I stand up here in front of a room full of people, I'm hoping all eyes are *not* on me, because the contempt on my face is unmaskable. *Is unmaskable a word?*

Anyway, believe me, I've tried and tried all morning to don a happy façade of a smile, but to no avail. I am standing up here pledging the rest of my life to a man who can't stand me, and his expression isn't any happier than mine.

But to be fair…I can't stand him, either.

Oh…ha, ha…you're probably wondering why I'm marrying a man who holds no affection for me, whatsoever. That's the only easy thing about this ridiculousness.

See, the man standing before me glaring at me with hate and loathing battling in those stunning pools of caramel is…or rather, *was* my best friend since birth. Our mothers were lifelong friends and, thus, making our fathers the best of friends, as well. My parents' contribution to the earth's population was myself and my older brothers, Anthony Jr. and Stephen. Callum's parents (Callum's the groom who's currently wishing a thousand deaths upon me) popped out his smug, arrogant, obnoxious, infuriating self along with his older brother, Timothy, and his older sister, Darlene.

Since Callum and I were the babies of the families and the same age, we were thrown together at the earliest of ages, and we became best friends.

Until we weren't anymore.

We shared our first day of pre-school, our first school bus ride, our first sport sign-up (it was soccer, by the way), our first broken bones (I broke my leg falling out of a tree and Callum broke his arm trying to catch me), our first school dance…well, we just shared a lot of firsts.

I know you're probably thinking we shared *that* first also, but we didn't. He lost his virginity to some skank who was already a junior in high school while he was still only in the eighth grade. I lost mine years later. As a matter a fact, it wasn't until my second year in college that I finally gave up the goods to the boy I had been dating for about a year. It wasn't anything to write home about, but at least I cared about the guy.

As Callum and I grew older, we still shared a lot. We kept in touch as much as we could, what with both of us going to different colleges, but we had become more private over the years. We didn't feel the need to share every little thing. We kept our personal relationship details private and glossed over who we were dating whenever one of us had met someone.

That came to a disastrous end three months ago when he came home to celebrate his graduation from law school. The party was small and cozy with only family in attendance. We celebrated until our parents went to sleep and our siblings passed out in a haze of alcohol.

Oh, and how I wish I could go back in time and pass out with said siblings, but I couldn't, and I can't.

*Nooooooo.* You want to know what *I* did?

I proceeded to drink my weight in liquor and, instead of throwing up and passing out like a good little alcoholic, I ended up in bed with my best friend.

Naked and doing things I still couldn't believe my body was capable of.

And because my ex-best friend was just as stupefied with drink as I was…you guessed it folks. We forgot to use condoms. I say condoms with an 's' because we didn't have sex just once and then come to our senses, full of shock and guilt, like normal people…*nooooooo,* we fucked *all goddamn night long.*

As you can guess, due to our minor lack of judgment, we ended up with a major problem. Yours truly got knocked up. And because the choices were an abortion (which…uh, no), adoption (see abortion insert), being a single momma (which I have no problem with, except it would destroy my parents' friendship with Callum's parents) and marrying the prick….

Well, you can figure it out since I am wearing this cursed wedding dress.

The funny thing is…this wasn't even my idea. The man currently banishing me to the depths of Hell in his mind, damn near forced this horrible, horrible idea on me. He said…and I'm quoting here, 'Our parents aren't going to suffer for our stupidity. So, you either marry me willingly or I'll drug you and find the shadiest preacher I can find to make this happen'.

*Yay!*

Not.

# CHAPTER 1

*Chloe*

I wasn't sure how much more of this I would be able to take.

I sat in a chair that was as far away from Callum as possible without it being too obvious that I didn't want to be anywhere near my newly acquired husband. I sat silently as I watched my parents and Callum's parents host the reception. Both fathers had given their speeches along with Callum's brother (since he was the Best Man and all). Both mothers cried and carried on.

Honestly, everyone seemed pretty happy and lively.

It was only Callum and I who were miserable and wishing to be anywhere else on the planet.

I was pissed because we had been so careless. He was pissed because he thinks I trapped him.

Pfft...*puhleeeease*...because out of all the men on the planet, *he* was the best candidate to trap into marriage. I mean, seriously, if I was all about trapping a man, it would have been one who wasn't annoying as fuckall.

I tried to point out several times that this marriage had been *his* idea, not mine, so how the hell is that *me* trapping *him?* I also tried to point out that I hadn't been appointed a court date to dispute charges of rape against his person. So, again, how is this *me* trapping *him?*

I did, however, almost end up with a court date to dispute assault charges when he said I should be responsible enough to...let me see, how exactly did he put it? Oh, yeah...'if you're going to spread your legs, you should have enough sense to be on birth control'. I almost cracked his skull in with my Donald Duck clock, but Donald hadn't deserved that kind of abuse.

Sooooooooo, my ex-best friend/new husband believes this is my entire fault, and that I had some long, thought out, nefarious plan to force his hand in marriage since we were born.

Can a man be more arrogant?

No...seriously...can he?

Well, the entire night hasn't been a complete disaster. We managed to get by with Callum kissing me softly on my cheek when the priest announced us husband and wife, and I was able to keep from having to hold his hand when I pretended I needed to use both my hands to gather my dress up as we walked down the aisle after our 'I dos'.

I had also lied to our mothers earlier and made up some fake ankle sprain that occurred as I was walking down the aisle and talked my way out of having to engage in the bride/groom first dance. I even got out of the cake eating when I pulled my mom aside and told her my stomach hurt and if she didn't want me spending the entire reception in the bathroom, she had better save me from the cake.

It worked.

She made up some nonsense about preserving the top tier, blah, blah, blah. All I cared about was that Callum didn't have a chance to shove cake in my face. I've no doubt he would have held it over my face until I died of suffocation. Then he could act the poor inconsolable groom/widow.

I just needed to get through one more hour and we could make our escapes. Sure, it sucked that we had to go back to his house together because it would look sketchy as hell if I spend our wedding night at my house, while he spent it at his, but oh well. We were still kind of at a standstill on where we were going to live, but I knew one of us would have to bite the bullet sooner rather than later.

"Come dance with me, Beautiful." I looked up into the sweet, blue eyes of Callum's best friend (now that I'd been replaced), Andrew McAlister. He was a good-looking piece of man meat, and maybe in another life, I'd have jumped on that, but not now.

You know…being married and all.

"I'd love to, but I hurt my left ankle earlier. It really hurts." I had to stick with the script.

He leaned in closer. "I bet I can take the weight off your ankle if I hold you really, really close." He winked at me and I melted just a little.

"Well, in that case, I'd love to, Andrew," I agreed.

I heard little gasps of shock as Andrew lifted me bride style and walked out onto the dance floor with me. I should probably feel embarrassed or ashamed that I was dancing with another man when I hadn't even danced with my groom, but…hey, the groom didn't offer to carry me out onto the dance floor. Plus, the groom was perfectly fine with not having to dance with me.

True to his word, Andrew wrapped his right arm around my waist and used his body to support mine. His left hand held my right one close, and he moved in a soft, slow circle making sure there was no weight on my left leg.

It was sweet, and I felt a smidge bad for lying, but not bad enough to tell him to put me down.

I rested my head on Andrew's shoulder and closed my eyes. "You smell nice," I pointed out.

I could hear and feel him chuckled. "Thanks, so do you."

After a few seconds-and because I'm no fool-I asked the obvious. "Why did you ask me to dance, Andrew?"

"Because you really are beautiful?" He posed his answer like a question.

I pulled my head back, so I could look at him. "Are you asking me or telling me?"

He sighed. "I know the real reason you guys got married, Chloe. I just wanted to tell you that despite...all that, to Callum, this is a real marriage." His face looked serious. It was almost as if he was expecting the worst from me and he hoped that this little speech of his would make a difference.

"I didn't know he confided all the dirty, little details to you." I was a little upset to be caught off guard like this, but I really wasn't surprised. Callum needed someone he could crucify me to.

"Chloe-"

"May I cut in?"

Andrew stopped turning me and we both froze at Callum's request. I'm not sure why Andrew froze, but I froze out of sheer shock and awe. Why in the hell would Callum want to cut in? Why?

*Is the boy nuts?*

"Of course, Cal. She is your wife after all," Andrew conceded.

"Good to know one of you still remembers that," Callum muttered.

I wanted to roll my eyes. I mean, how could I not? He was being stupid and ridiculous. But because I was a grownup, I managed not to roll my eyes, and I allowed Callum to take me into his arms.

The peace lasted all of three seconds. "You can stop with your fake sprained ankle bullshit now, Chloe."

"No. No, actually I can't. I told that fake story to too many people. I'm riding that lie out until I can get the hell out of here," I retorted. I could actually hear his teeth grinding and a brilliant idea popped into my head. "I'm going to wince, reached down and grab my fake injured ankle and you will gallantly assist me back to my chair. This way we don't have to-"

He threw his head back and laughed. Now, to everyone else, it might look like he is enjoying himself and was happy as a ham to have me in his arms, but I knew better.

Remember...best friends since birth until the ex-best friends' debacle.

"So, you're perfectly fine with braving the pain to dance with Andrew, but it's not worth suffering to dance with your husband?" Callum hissed in my ear.

"Oh, believe me when I tell you I'm suffering tremendously right now," I hissed back.

"Don't make me murder you on your wedding day, Chloe," he threatened.

"Pfft, please...it would take someone with compassion to put me out of my misery, so talk about an empty threat."

He laughed again. "Well, if I'm going to be miserable for the rest of my life, then so the fuck are you." Callum squeezed my body tighter. "I'm going to spend every single day making sure you're as miserable as I am. You're going to regret ever opening your legs for some convenient dick."

*Wow.*

Now, I get that people tend to get nasty when their upset or have had their feelings hurt, etc. But this was too much by comparison. He's really acting liking I took advantage of him in his drunken state and purposely got pregnant.

*The no good, cocksucking, sonofabitch.*

I hit back, because I wasn't going to take his shit like a weak-willed pussy. "No way I'll regret it, Callum. The way I see it, I can now fuck any *convenient* random dick I come across because I can't get knocked up twice. I mean, really…this mistake with you is rather quite liberating."

I felt him step on my foot so hard I gasped and reached down in pain. He stepped back and then scooped me up, holding me close to him. From the outside looking in, it appeared as if he was a concerned groom taking care of his new bride.

That was *so not* the case.

His next words were proof that it was step on my toe or strangle me in front of our parents and wedding guests. He nuzzled his face into the crook of my neck as he walked me off the dance floor. "Make no mistake, Chloe. I will torture you in ways your mind will not be able to comprehend, right before I kill you if you ever betray your wedding vows to me."

And because I wasn't ready to be the mature one and because Callum was acting like a world class prick, I responded cheekily, "You actually remember our wedding vows?" I shrugged a shoulder. "I guess you'll have to write them down for me. I tend to forget meaningless gibberish."

I thought he was going to threaten me with more bodily harm, but instead, he threw me off balance when he quietly whispered, "God, I can't believe how much I hate you."

I'm not going to lie. His words cause my eyes to gloss over. It was because I knew, in this moment, he meant every word of that sentence. Callum, the kid who used to play with me, the boy who used to protect me, the guy that used to confide in me, the man who used to know me is now the husband who hates his wife with unrivaled distaste.

*Me.*

I lost a lot of my childhood when I lost Callum. All I thought we had meant to each other vanished when he accused me of getting pregnant on purpose. The fact that he thought I would actually do something so underhanded to him had first shocked me and then hurt me.

He dumped me back in my chair as he took his seat next to me. I kept my head down because I didn't want him to see how painful his words were.

"Are you okay, Slater?" I almost lost it at my new best friend's words. Mya

Carlson became my best friend during our sophomore year in college. She was 5'5" with locks like melted gold and brilliant blue eyes. She was smart, funny, beautiful, and the most nonjudgmental person I knew. Mya was open, honest and never meant anyone any harm.

I absolutely loved her, and I couldn't think of anyone better to be my Maid of Honor for this ceremony of Hell and Damnation. I looked up at her sitting next to me and I couldn't stop the tears from falling. "I need to get out of here, Mya," I whispered.

The reason I didn't hold any real resentment at Callum for confiding in Andrew was because I had spilled everything to Mya as it was happening. She knew what had happened between me and Callum that night and why we were married now.

I knew I could count on her.

She immediately bent down and acted like she was examining my foot. She sat up and turned to my mother. "Mrs. Slater, we need to get Chloe out of here. Her ankle looks really bad."

My mother looked over at me and could see the tears in my eyes. "Oh, Chloe, honey, I didn't realize it was that bad." She then turned towards my dad sitting on the other side of her. "Anthony, we need to help get Chloe home. She's hurt."

I saw my father look around my mother at me. His furrowed his brow. "What about Callum? Why wouldn't he be taking her home?"

I leaned forward as much as I could in hopes that the man in question couldn't hear me. "It's his wedding reception. He shouldn't have to leave the party because of me, Dad."

My father's brows went from pulled together to riding high on his forehead. "Why would he want to stay here without his bride to celebrate with?"

I shrugged a shoulder. "He's having a good time. I just don't want to spoil it for him, is all."

"That's the most ridiculous thing I've ever heard of, Chloe," he gruffed.

"Dad, please. My ankle hurts really bad and I just want to get out of here."

He looked like he wanted to argue, but he had three forlorn female faces staring him down, and even if Mya and I weren't in the mix, my dad was a sucker for my mother. "Fine, sweetie, let's get you home. Callum can…" He took a deep breath. "Let's just get you home."

All four of us stood up at the same time and Callum looked up as my father came around and wrapped his right arm around my shoulder. "Chloe's not well, Callum. We're taking her home, son."

I had turned my body into my father's-yeah, I know, super cowardly-so I didn't have to face Callum as my family rescued me. So, I wasn't prepared for the steel in his voice to sound so cold. "I appreciate you trying to take care of her Mr. Slater, but that's my job now. I'll take her home."

Mya jumped in like the best friend she was. "It's cool, Callum. We don't want to take you away from the party. We can get Slater home." Ever since I told Chloe about Callum's reaction to the pregnancy, she's been calling me Slater in front of him just to drive the point home that this wasn't a real marriage.

As sweet as Mya was, she didn't take to kindly to Callum's accusation of entrapment.

"Rosewood," he corrected her.

"What?"

Callum stood up and stepped passed me and got into Mya's face. "Her name is Rosewood," he hissed at her. "Chloe Rosewood, *not* Slater."

That one sentence gave me the courage to pull away from my father's arms. I stepped into Callum's personal space. I waited until he looked down and focused all of his hate on me before I spoke, "I will always be a Slater and I'm keeping my last name to make sure of it."

## CHAPTER 2

*Callum*

Chloe Slater was the only female in my history of females to be able to make me feel every emotion known to man all at once.

I absolutely hated her.

Almost as much as I loved her.

And if she thought she was going to keep going by Chloe Slater, she was out of her fucking mind. She was always meant to carry my last name. I felt it when I was 10 years old and I knew it when I was 14. I just never thought it'd come about because she'd get pregnant.

I peered down at her, ignoring the stares from her parents and Mya. "Over my dead body, will you keep going by Slater," I threatened.

"Now, Callum…" Mr. Slater started to inject.

"It's okay, Dad," Chloe jumped in. "I was just being silly. You know, trying to avoid the DMV lines and all." She tried to laugh it off, and I knew she was only doing it to keep her father from wondering what was really going on between us.

He turned his gaze away from mine and looked over at Chloe and chuckled. "Good to hear, Chloe. You know I don't like all this new age crap where women don't take on their husbands' names. If Callum's expected to take care of you, then he should get the credit for doing so. And he gets credit every time you introduce yourself as Chloe Rosewood. Remember that, honey."

I noticed her eyes tear up and a lone drop cascaded down her cheek. I'd give my left nut to know what she was thinking in this moment. But she simply replied, "I know, Dad."

I couldn't help the glare I shot Mya's way when she piped up. "Okay, well, I'm sure Chloe's ankle isn't going to be able to take much more, so let's get her out of here, yeah?"

I knew that Mya knew Chloe was faking it and it burned to know she was trying to help Chloe escape our wedding reception. Chloe didn't deserve a reprieve. She let me fuck her-repeatedly-without letting me know that she wasn't protected. She deserved to fucking suffer.

See, the plan had always been simple. After graduating at the top of my class at Harvard, I was hired by Clayton, Nelson & Moreno, one of the most prestigious law firms in California. I was going to work there for about a year, until I had all my ducks in a row, and then marry Chloe and start a family.

It wouldn't have matter if she would have been dating someone else at the time or not. Chloe was mine. She had always been mine and was meant to always be mine.

When she graduated college, she had come back home and started working for Sans Publishing in their finance department. Chloe had a bachelor's in finance and accounting with a minor in literature. She was already settled in her career and set. The plan was just waiting for me to finish up law school.

And then she had to go and get fucking pregnant.

So, instead of marrying me because she loved me and because I have always loved her, we got married to preserve our parents' friendship and do the right thing by our child. And, no matter whose fault it was, I wasn't going to walk away from my responsibilities.

But my blood burned like acid in my veins knowing she would never believe I married her because I loved her. She will always believe I asked her…well, *told* her…because she got pregnant. I resented her getting pregnant because it ruined all my plans.

She had me.

Chloe always had me. She didn't have to trap me!

"As much as, I'm sure, Chloe appreciates your concern, Mya, I'll be taking her home and looking after her," I assured her.

Mya shot me a look of pure loathing. While Andrew felt pity over my situation, Mya felt anger over it. She made no secret of the fact that she didn't think Chloe should have to tie herself to me for life just because of one night. And I knew she called Chloe by her last name just to irritate the fuck out of me. Her voice dripped with contempt, "If her wellbeing is such a priority for you, then might I suggest you get her home and argue over a piddly name change later, once she feels better?"

"Mya-"

I wrapped my arm around Chloe's waist and hauled her away from her father. A groan almost escaped my lips as my body immediately recognized hers. Hell, I had to step on her goddamn foot and carry her off the dance floor before she felt the raging hard-on I was sporting when I held her close for our dance.

I goddamn hated this woman, but my body fucking *craved* her.

I stared Mya down. "You're right." I looked over at Mr. and Mrs. Slater. "Please make our excuses and tell my mom and dad that Chloe needed to come first."

Mrs. Slater tittered, "Oh, how sweet. Of course, we'll let Mark and Gina know why you left."

It would have been extremely easy to just walk the few steps over to where my parents sat, but my nerves were already frayed, and I wanted to just hurry up and get the fuck out of here before Chloe snapped and confessed all.

Chloe looked up at me, her delicate hands wrapped around each of my biceps. "Callum, you don't have to leave the party. My parents and Mya can help m-"

It was just a threat earlier, but I think she really was trying to get me to murder her on our wedding day. "You're *mine*, Chloe," I reminded her. "That means *I* take care of you."

She pursed her lips together, and I knew she was doing all she could not to swing at me. Chloe was fucking stunning, always has been. And I looked down at her, taking in her rich, soft, luxurious chocolate tresses and her dark, ocean blue eyes, surrounded by long, full lashes. Her brows were perfectly arched and feminine. Her nose delicate and perfectly centered on a face made up of rosy, round cheeks and full, soft lips. Lips that I can still picture wrapped around my cock.

But what stood out the most was the scar that slashed across her right cheekbone.

When we were eight, we were sword fighting with some twigs in my parents' backyard, and she was taunting me and driving me so insane, I lunged for her with the twig in my hand and I accidentally sliced her face open.

I'll never forget the sight of her blood pouring down her cheek and the panic and fear that gripped my throat at the knowledge that I had hurt her.

*Really* hurt her.

When she came running towards me, I had thought she was running towards me so I could save her and make everything better, but I was wrong.

I was so very, very wrong.

I was so consumed with worry, about what I had done to her, I hadn't notice she still had a twig in her hand.

Chloe charged at me, knocked me down and sliced the twig across my face. And as a result, we sported the same scar on the exact same cheek.

And so, because I had no doubt that Chloe wasn't afraid to slug me at our own wedding reception, I knew I needed to get her out of here before this turned into a Jerry Springer episode. "Let's go," I said before picking her up bride-style and heading out of the reception hall.

She wrapped her arms around my neck-probably afraid I would drop her-and held on tight, with her head cushioned under my neck. Anyone looking at us would think they were looking at an affectionate bride and groom making their getaway to a long-awaited wedding night.

Nope.

Instead, we were two people who resented each other and the position we were in. Sure, we had no one else to blame but ourselves, but that didn't make the situation any easier.

As I carried Chloe to the limo, all I could think about was how pissed I was at how gloriously she fit in my arms. Inside I was a rage of hate and heat at knowing what her body felt like and what her secrets tasted like.

Her mouth tasted like sweet fruit, her skin tasted like her cherry blossom lotion, her tits tasted like fucking ambrosia and her pussy tasted like heavenly addiction. And all I would have were the memories of it all.

There was no way Chloe was going to let me near her now and, truthfully, I didn't know if I would be able to stand being near her. As her stomach grew, I didn't know if I would be able to welcome the changes to her body or resent the intrusion more.

She was carrying my child, and I knew I was going to love that child more than my own life. I just didn't know if he or she would be able to bring us together or be the thing that kept us apart.

I had every intention of being a great father, but I had no desire to be a good husband.

Let me rephrase that.

I had no desire to be a good *fake* husband.

And that's what Chloe and I were. I was a fake husband to a fake wife.

I placed her in the back of the limo, and I climbed in after her, my dark thoughts taking over. And just when I thought I could push them back, Chloe had to go and open her big, goddamn mouth.

"I'm not changing my last name to Rosewood," she stated firmly, while looking out the tinted window. "It's too much of a hassle since I'll be changing it back to Slater someday."

Her hint at our predestined divorce nearly had me reaching over to strangle her.

# CHAPTER 3

*Chloe*

We rode the limo back to Callum's apartment in silence.

I didn't know what he was pissed about, but I was pissed over all that bullshit about how I was his and it was his job to take care of me. I mean, I knew he was putting on a show for my parents, but still.

A small part of me had wanted his words to be true, but that was stupid since all the other parts of me wanted to beat his head in with a shovel and bury him a Louisiana swamp. I had to nix that idea though, because I couldn't smuggle a dead body on a plane, and I didn't think I could take enough time off work to make the drive there and back.

Plus, I didn't have the money to bribe a swamp tour guide to look the other way as I made Callum alligator food.

*Oh, how I envied the rich.*

Plus, I didn't like the way he tried to intimidate Mya. He had Andrew, so I was allowed to have Mya. And just because Andrew seemed more accepting of the situation than any of us, didn't mean Mya had to turn the other cheek when Callum was being a dick.

Callum's voice was like gravel as he brought me out of my homicidal fantasy. "Look, Chloe, I get that you live in a world where you can talk to unicorns and leprechauns are your friends..." *Did this asshole just call me crazy?* "...but you're even crazier than I thought if you think I'll ever let you divorce me."

Yep. This arrogant douchewad just called me crazy.

My first instinct was to push him out of the moving limousine, but I opted for some truth instead. "I plan on starting divorce proceedings six months before this kid turns 18 and heads off to college," I informed him, snidely. "That way, I can throw him/her a graduation party and throw myself a freedom party, all in the same weekend."

I was staring out the window, taking in the scenery and that's the reason I missed his oncoming attack. I mean, not that I could have really warded it off, being trapped in the limo with him and all, but…

Callum's arm shot out and his hand gathered a fist full of lace, silk and fluff, dragging me across the seat until half of my body was lying across his lap and he had both my arms in the grip of his hands.

A hard grip.

His brilliant russet gaze bore into mine. "I get that 'ever' being a two-syllable word might make it hard for you to understand," he snapped. "So, I'll make it a little more clearer for you. When that kid is 60 years old, you're still going to be married to me, understood?"

*God, why did his insulting words make me wish he'd kiss me?*

What a goddamn clusterfuck.

I tried for bravado. "We got married to raise this child together, Callum. Once it's raised, there will be no reason for us to still have to torture each other," I reminded him.

I could see the muscle in his jaw tick, and he looked even more pissed off than before. "And what about the other kids?" he asked in a voice full of gruff and anger.

I blinked.

And I blinked again, because…*what the hell?*

What *other* children?

There were other children in this futuristic hellhole?

"What are you talking about?" I finally asked. "What *other* kids?"

He scoffed, like I was the biggest idiot on the planet. "Do you honestly believe I'm only going to have one child?" he asked, answering my question with a question.

I shook my head in shock at his implication. "Wh…what d…do you mean?"

"Don't act stupid, Chloe," he spat. "You've always known I wanted at least three kids."

My eyes rounded in disbelief. "But…but that was…was when you were going to be married to someone you loved," I reasoned. I mean, there's no way he could be talking about having more kids with me. That would bind us together longer and entwine our lives even more. The more children we had, the more weddings we'd have to attend, the more grandchildren we'd have, etc.

We would never be free from each other.

*Never.*

"No," he said snapping me out of the vision of my dismal future. "I always wanted children with my *wife*," Callum shook my body for emphasis, "and that just so happens to be *you*."

I didn't say it, but if he wanted more children, then that meant he'd have to sleep with me again. And if he wanted two more that meant he'd have to sleep with me at least two more times.

I didn't think I could handle that.

Over the years, I watched as Callum grew from a cute kid, to a lanky boy, to a hot guy, to a sexy as fuck man and now knowing what he was capable of in between the sheets…I didn't think I could survive another night in bed with him.

Callum was 6'2" of all hard male. He had dark brown hair that always looked like some woman should be running her fingers through it. His matching brown eyes were intense and scorching. His brows sat perfectly over each eye and his face was made up of masculine angles and a rough five o'clock shadow if he didn't shave every day.

And his body…*Jesus Christ, his body.*

Underneath those tailored attorney suits was a body of wide shoulders, a smooth chest and big, muscular tatted up arms. His chest tapered down to a waist that boasted of a six-pack with dents so deep, my tongue had gotten lost in them when I trailed my way down his body that night. He had hard, defined hips that flowed into a pair of strong thighs and legs that held me up in the most straining of sexual positions. *And his dick…*

Eight inches of unbelievable thickness that had left me sore and dreaming of more.

My reminiscing almost had me in tears when I realized there was no telling the next time I was going to be able to have sex. I couldn't have it with my husband, and even though this was a fake marriage, and I had said as much at the reception, I didn't really know if I could sleep with another man while I was married to Callum. Hell, while I was married *period.*

The limo came to a stop, putting a pause on the conversation. And even though I didn't know the driver personally, Callum and I sacrificed our happiness to make this marriage seem believable. I wasn't going to ruin it by arguing in front of a stranger and having there be a possibility that it would get back to our parents.

I scrambled out of Callum's hold and went for my freedom. I opened the door, and I was tumbling out before the limo driver had even shut his door. I jumped to my feet as gracefully as I could, and I honestly didn't care if the dress got ruined or not. It wasn't a real wedding therefore; this wasn't a real wedding dress.

"Ma'am, are you okay," the driver asked as he scurried his way over towards me.

I held up a hand to hold him back. "I'm fine. Perfectly fine," I assured him. Other than being in a loveless marriage to a man that couldn't stand the sight of me…other than that, I was fine.

Callum made his way around the back of the limo and just stood there looking at me. He was staring at me as if he was trying to figure me out, but what was there to figure out? He's known me since we were born. He knew me better than anyone.

Or, so, I thought, because this *was* the same man who thought I was the type of woman to get pregnant on purpose.

He shook his head as if I wasn't worth the effort anymore and headed towards his apartment, leaving me to trail after him.

It was rude, insulting and dismissing.

*God, I hated him.*

But I followed, because what the hell else was I going to do? I dredged up the stairs and saw that he left the door wide open for me.

*How sweet.*

I entered his apartment and shut the door behind me thinking 'now what'. I stood in the middle of his living room because I had no idea where to go or what to do.

Callum had snagged one of the most coveted apartments in one of the most prominent neighborhoods in Branston. Branston was located on the outskirts of San Jose, California and was a very nice town, with enough city to it to make it comfortable.

The apartment building boasted of ten floors and his apartment was on the top floor. It had an open living plan where the living room and kitchen were a shared space. The living room had a floor to ceiling window that looked out onto the town and the kitchen shown bright with all stainless-steel appliances and a granite island that was the only place for eating.

It had a master suite with a private bathroom and walk-in closet. It was down the hall and took up the entire left side of the floor. On the right side of the hallway, you could find two other bedrooms that were separated by a full bathroom. The bedroom at the end of the hall was a guest bedroom and the other bedroom had been converted into a home office.

Back when Callum and I had been friends, I was the first person he had given a tour to, and I had fallen in love with every inch of the place. But now that I was an obvious intruder, the apartment felt stifling.

Callum was nowhere to be seen, so I assumed he went off to his bedroom, and I looked around lost, wondering what I was going to do. It was then that I remembered I didn't even have a change of clothes with me. I honestly hadn't thought this through. For some reason, I thought Callum would go to his apartment and I would go off to mine. I seriously didn't think to bring an overnight bag or anything.

It was a few seconds later when Callum emerged from the hallway dressed in a crimson Harvard t-shirt, dark black jeans and black Timberlands to match. From a tuxedo to jeans and he looked just as gorgeous in both.

It wasn't fair.

I had plain brown hair, unremarkable blue eyes, and a marred face. While his scar made him look dangerous and dashing, mine had made me look deformed.

And his body next to mine was a joke.

I had to *wrestle* my way into this stupid wedding gown. I was 5'2" with enough excess on my body to cross over to chubby on a nice day, but fat during my periods. My chest was one cupcake away from becoming a D cup, and my waist was pulled in, but soft and would roll if I didn't sit just right. There was no question if my hips could bear children or not and my thighs kissed each other all the time. My legs were as long as my 5'2" would allow and my feet were functional and not at all sexy.

It just wasn't fair.

And I felt absolutely ridiculous standing in Callum's living room wearing a stupid wedding dress when he was dressed in his casual wear.

His gaze skimmed down my body and back up again before he asked, "Did you need help getting that thing off?"

*That thing?*

What a fucking prick.

"No," I snapped back, even though I really didn't know. It took a team of Mya, my mother and Callum's mother to smuggle me into this contraption, I honestly didn't know if I'd be able to get myself out of it alone. But I refused to ask him for help. I'd cut myself out of the damn thing first, before I admitted I needed his help with anything.

"Then why are you just standing there still wearing it?"

God, I wanted to stab him to death. But I was only 26 years old. I did not want to spend the rest of my life in prison. So, again, curbing my homicidal fantasies, I went with the truth. "I forgot to bring an overnight bag. I don't have anything else to wear," I admitted.

He ran his hand through his hair like my lack of clothing options was such a major frustration for him. "Jesus Christ, Cee," he swore, and my heart lurched. We used to call each other Cee back when we were friends.

*It must have been just a slip of the tongue.*

"Look, I'll just call an Uber and go back to my place," I said, hurt and frustrated.

He placed his hands on his hips regarding me like I was an errant child. "Seriously?" he asked. "And if someone sees you?"

"No one will see me. They're probably still all at the reception getting drunk and whatever," I reasoned.

He let out an awful laugh devoid of any hint of happiness. "You know what, Chloe, do whatever you want. Go ahead and call a fucking Uber."

*Christ on a surfboard, what did I do now?*

"What the hell is your problem?" I snapped at him. "I'm the one stuck in this godawful gown with nothing to wear, not you."

His eyes narrowed, and I could actually see his face heat with fury. "You want to know what my problem is? Okay, you asked," he warned. "My problem is *you*, Chloe. Plain and simple, *just you*," he swiped at me as he grabbed his jacked off the back of the couch.

His words sliced at me, but that didn't stop me from asking, "Where are you going?"

"Out," he barked.

"What do you mean out?" I asked, my voice rising in octaves. "And if someone sees *you?*"

Callum stopped at the door and turned back to face me. It's a moment I'll never forget for the rest of my life. The look on his face. The hate in the air. The tension in our bodies. "It's my wedding night, Chloe. I'm going to go spend it getting my dick wet like any normal groom should." My eyes widened at his hateful, hurtful words. "Don't wait up," he said turning the doorknob behind him. "As a matter of fact, why don't you just stay at your place once you get over there. There's no need for you here." Callum slammed the door behind him, leaving me standing in the middle of his living room alone.

The weight on my chest felt real.

The pressure in the back of my eyes pulsed.

My husband was going to spend his first night as a married man fucking another woman.

*Awesome.*

## CHAPTER 4

*Callum*

I regretted the words the second they finished leaving my lips. And shame swallowed me whole the second I slammed the door behind me, leaving her standing alone, her face full of anguish.

But what did I do?

I kept walking.

I kept walking because I didn't know how to make this right.

Walking out of my bedroom, I was able to see her standing in the living room and I hated that she looked lost. I hated that she looked uncomfortable in my home. I hated that she didn't know how to behave.

*I fucking hated it.*

It was the first time that she'd been in my apartment since she told me she was pregnant, and until tonight, all the memories of Chloe in my home were of her lying on the couch with her feet propped up on the coffee table, switching back between football and baseball, and stuff like that. The images were endless of her in my kitchen cooking, of her drunk passed out on the couch, of her asleep in my bed-because she was too good for the guest room.

She had fallen in love with the apartment when I first moved in, and now, she looked like she would rather sleep in the sewers than spend one night under my roof.

I dialed Andrew because I was on the verge of throwing myself off a random overpass. "Callum?"

"Where are you?" I asked without any niceties whatsoever.

"Still at your reception," he laughed. "It's a hell of a party, dude. You're missing out," he joked.

"Can you meet me at Ribicci's?" I was already in my car, turning on the ignition.

"Whoa, wait. What do you mean meet you at Ribicci's?" he asked, stunned.

I didn't blame him for his incredulousness. Ribicci's was a strip club on the outskirts of town going into the seedier side of San Jose. "Just what I said," I retorted, impatiently. "I'll be there in about 20 minutes or so."

He must have gone off to somewhere private, because the background noise diminished when he finally said, "Jesus Christ, Callum. Please do not tell me you are seriously thinking of spending your wedding night at a fucking strip club?" His voice sounded like I had just told him I was going to spend the evening kidnapping random neighborhood pets and setting them on fire.

I closed my eyes and I could feel the pressure in the back of my head make its way towards the front. "I need to do something, Andrew. And that something is to get rip-roaring drunk so I can forget this fucked up situation. And maybe, just maybe, if I'm drunk enough, I can pretend one of those disposable whores at Ribicci's is Chloe and I can get some pussy tonight. It is my wedding night, after all," I reminded him, sarcastically.

"Callum, I need you to listen to me, man. You need to go back to Chloe and undo whatever it is you just did," he stressed, his voice full of desperation.

"What if I don't want to?" I knew it was a lie. I wanted to. I wanted to remove that look from her face, so badly. I wanted to drop to my knees and beg for forgiveness.

Then stay down there and eat her pussy.

Andrew's voice took on a hard edge, "Look, Callum, you can feed that bullshit to whoever else you want. Hell, you can even feed it to yourself, but I know you. I know you, and I remember every word you've ever said about that girl. She might not know you're in love with her, and you might wish you weren't, but we both know that you are. And I know why you're so pissed, and I get it, I really do. But I also know that if you go out and get so drunk you end up fucking some random piece of ass, you're going to want to hang yourself in the morning."

"Andr-"

"Are you honestly going to tell me you hate Chloe so much to the point where you would humiliate her by cheating on her on your fucking wedding day?" he asked, astonished at the possibility. "Because if you do hate her that much, and you really want to be with another woman while Chloe is still in her wedding dress, then please, for the love of God, file for an annulment on Monday and walk away before you guys end up killing each other," he pleaded.

My chest felt like it was caving in. My entire body ran cold as he suggested an annulment. "What if I can't make it right?" I asked, voicing my true fear.

The look on her face. Jesus Christ.

"Anything else is better than what you're contemplating, Callum," he stated simply.

"I feel like I'm going crazy, Andrew," I admitted. I feel like my emotions and my thoughts are in the battle of their lives and they were both losing.

"You gotta tell her the truth, man," he advised for the millionth time.

I turned off the ignition and got out of my car. I knew I couldn't go anywhere, but I couldn't go back up to the apartment just yet. I wasn't sure if I could face her. That had been a shit thing to say to her even by asshole standards.

I walked out of the underground parking garage and stood on the side of the building, breathing in some fresh air. I really felt like I was going insane.

"Callum…" Andrew's voice became static when I saw Chloe coming out of the building, holding the rim of her wedding dress, walking towards an idling car by the curb.

Jesus, she really did call an Uber to take her home.

My first thought was that she didn't have her purse on her. Was he going to give her trouble when she had to go into her apartment to get money? Was this stranger going to insist on following her up, so she doesn't stiff him?

For some reason-even with all the shitty things I have said and have done to her tonight-the idea of her leaving in an Uber with no money made me feel lower than low.

"I have to go, Andrew," I said as I hung up on him. I ran and reached the car just as she was closing the door. The fact that she had to gather all the material from her dress had bought me enough time to stop the door from shutting. She looked up at me and her face almost dropped me to my knees.

Her eyes were bloodshot and the rims red. Her skin was blotchy, and her lips trembled. Her face looked perfectly heartbroken, but it only lasted a few seconds. The second she realized it was me holding her up, her blue eyes turned to ice and her entire body locked up for a fight. "Move," she seethed.

"Do…do you have money for…" I felt like a goddamn fool. I felt like the worst kind of failure.

Her eyes were so full of hate and contempt, I could actually see the emotions swirling in her blue depths. "I called Mya using your landline and she paid for it on her Uber account. Now move, or I swear to God, I will tell him to run you over," she swore.

"Chloe…" I tried again, still holding the door open.

"Goddamn it, move!" she screamed. "I swear to God, Callum, you have two seconds to shut this door or I swear on all that is holy, I will tell everyone everything!"

I shut the door and jumped back out of the way.

Not because I was a coward, but because if she told our parents everything, then she wouldn't have to stay married to me. If she came clean with them, then they would force us all to sit down and figure it all out, and the result wouldn't necessarily leave me with Chloe.

But I couldn't leave things like this.

I couldn't let her go back to her apartment believing that I was spending our wedding night with another woman.

I can't believe I spewed those words just to hurt her, and all because I couldn't get my shit together and look past her deliberate pregnancy.

What a fucking asshole I am.

How could I say those words to her, especially when Andrew was right? There's no way I could ever go through with something like that. I always knew Chloe was going to be it for me, but once I knew what it felt like to be inside her, it was over. No other woman on the planet could tempt me, knowing what I had in Chloe.

If her perfect face wasn't enough-if that scar that bound us together wasn't enough-her body was the sexiest, most luscious landscape I have ever seen. I knew she thought she was chubby and overweight, but I never thought so. Throughout our childhood, she always wore shorts and a t-shirt when we went swimming and I hated that she didn't see herself the way I saw her.

But that night of my graduation, the night I had finally seen her completely naked and in heat, all my fantasies about her paled in comparison to the real thing. Chloe was all woman and I couldn't get enough of her that night. I thought in our drunken states, we'd pass out after the first time, satisfied and spent, but we didn't. We went at one another each time like we at war with each other.

Her tits bounced in time with each of my thrusts into her body. Her flesh molded to my hands perfectly. Her ass rippled in waves with every push of my cock and every slap of my hand. Her thighs held me tight to her body. And her face...God, her face, I wanted to watch her face as she came for the rest of my life.

The sight was absolutely stunning.

I knew I was fucking this up something serious, but I didn't know how to make it right. If I told her I loved her she wouldn't believe me, and I was not going to have my first and only declaration of love not be taken seriously.

Chloe would always think I married her because she got pregnant and I didn't want to upset our parents, and it'd be partly true. I did marry her today for those reasons, but I would have married her a year from now for other reasons. Primarily, because I've loved her my whole life.

I ran back to my car after the Uber sped away and followed them. I was beyond stupid and cruel to tell her I was going to be fucking someone else tonight, and if I had to camp out on her couch to prove I didn't mean it, I would.

Hell, if I had to sleep outside in my car to prove it, I would. Because-let's face it-the odds of her letting me sleep on her couch were slim to none. I'd be lucky if she even opened the door for me.

And while I admit, I've been a complete asshole, I still can't wrap my mind around the fact that she let herself get pregnant. Yeah, we were stupid drunk that night, but not once did she mention she wasn't on birth control. If she had, I would have...well, I probably still would have jumped her, but at least I would have known what I was getting myself into. I would have told her that night how much I loved her, and she would have believed me.

When I finally pulled in front of her apartment complex, I didn't see her anywhere, but I got caught behind a couple of red traffic lights, so she was probably already in her apartment. Chloe lived on the third floor and the damn elevator was always broken, so I had to waste more time jogging up the damn stairs to get to her.

My heart started pounding inside my chest when I finally stood in front of the door to her apartment. I knocked on her door seriously praying the night wouldn't end with one of her neighbors calling the cops. The door swung open and all the breath left my body. "This damn corset is worse than the…what the fuck are you doing here?" Chloe screeched, and then she popped her head out into the hallway, looking side to side. She took a step back into her apartment and eyed me like she just caught me kicking a basket full of puppies. "Where's Mya?" she asked as if I was hiding Mya captive somewhere.

I wanted to say I didn't know, but my mouth was dry, and my lips wouldn't cooperate. Chloe was standing in front of me wearing nothing but a white corset that held up matching white stockings. Her tits were pushed up, begging for attention and a pathetic scrap of white lace barely covered her trimmed triangle of curls.

The sharpness in her voice snapped me back to reality. "I repeat, where is Mya? And what the hell are you doing here, Callum?"

I had to clear my throat twice before I could gather enough spit to make my mouth work. "I don't know where Mya is, but-"

"She said she was on her way and I need her to help me get this goddamn thing off me. It's burning my skin," she illogically claimed.

"Well, I'll say it again, I don't know where she is, but I could help you with-"

Her eyes rounded, and I saw the flex in her arm a fraction of a second before she went to slam the door in my face. But thanks to that tiny, miniscule flex, I was prepared. The door came flying my way, and I braced my hand against it, propelling it back. I stormed inside before she could try to shut it in my face again. "What do you think you're doing?" she yelled, her hands planted on those drool worthy hips of hers.

"Can you, please, go put some clothes on so we can talk?" I answered, when I really wanted to tell her to go put some clothes on before the last of my restraint snapped and I fucked her on her living room floor.

Her face was magnificent in her anger. "How 'bout you get the hell out of my house, Callum," she bit out. "How about that?"

"Go get dressed," I countered with barely enough resolve to get me through those three words.

"I can't, you asshole! Didn't you just hear me say I needed Mya to help me out of this piece of misery?" That's when I noticed the front of the corset was smooth and lacey. That meant the hooks were in the back.

*Motherfucker.*

At this point, I had two choices. I could torture myself by talking to her while she wore that goddamn thing, or I could torture myself by helping her take it off.

Fuck. My. Life.

Frustration and anger at my own damn indecisiveness had me barking at her. "Well, then, turn the fuck around so I can unhook the damn thing and you can go get dressed." I moved towards her. "We need to talk."

She was still standing with her hands on her hips, looking at me like I was the Antichrist. "I'll be able to manage," she retorted. "What are you doing here, Callum? Don't you have some pussy you should be balls deep in right now? Oh, wait, are you here to borrow some condoms? I mean, because we both know how you like to fuck random bitches unprotected," she spat.

Chloe was wearing my ring and carrying my child and she just referred to herself as some random bitch I fucked without protection.

Congratulations!

Resolved snapped.

# CHAPTER 5

*Chloe*

I've known Callum my entire life

*Soooooo,* I should have noticed the signs of his mind unraveling, but I didn't. Of course-to be fair-I've never seen his mind unravel before, so I'm not sure I would have even noticed had I been paying attention.

But I was paying attention now.

Callum had me by my shoulders and my back up against the wall right next to the front door. "Just so we're clear," he snarled in my face. "I have *never* had sex without a condom before you. I've never trusted a woman enough when she said she was protected. And it looks like I was right to think like that because the first and *only* woman I trusted with my bare dick is now fucking pregnant. *Isn't she?*"

"Fuck you, Callum," I flung at him, when I really wanted to sock the holy snot out of him.

"Oh, believe me, I'm well and truly fucked. You don't have to keep wishing that on me," he flung back. "And don't ever refer to yourself as some random bitch I fucked without protection again." He really leaned down and got in my face to deliver that gem. "You are my *wife* and the mother of my child. You are not some random piece of ass!"

I was angry and hurt.

I continuously felt angry and hurt where Callum was concerned, and the hate I felt towards Callum threatened to take me under. But the shame that traveled through my body had me acting reckless and destructive. I felt an overwhelming sense of shame, that after everything Callum's done to me since I told him I was pregnant, I still wanted him to strip me naked and make me forget that we hated each other. "Yeah, I get that. Because if I *was* a random piece of ass, you'd be fucking me right now instead wishing me to hell," I threw back in his face.

In a voice that could freeze fire, he said, "Be careful, Chloe, or I just might think you *want* me to fuck you."

And because I wanted to hurt him the way he hurt me, I responded in kind. "Just because I might want to be fucked, doesn't mean I want to be fucked by *you*, Callum. If you can be with other women, despite being legally married, well, then I can be with other men." I stood at my full height to back up how serious I sounded. "And I'm going to use this pregnancy to fuck as many men as I can without consequences before I start showing."

Callum's left hand slapped the wall next to my head, while his other hand wrapped around my throat, pinning me up against the wall. I'd never seen him look so livid in all our 26 years. He looked like he was going to murder me and his grip on my neck made me think that he just might. We were saying the most horrendous shit to each other, and it was bringing out the worst in both of us.

His eyes were all hell and damnation, and his voice was all jagged glass when he said, "You let another man touch you and he won't live to ever do it again, Chloe. You are *mine*. Whether you like it or not, whether *I* like it or not, you are *fucking mine*."

I couldn't contain my hurt feelings anymore and I hated myself for my weakness. "Then why would you suggest going to someone else?!"

"Because I didn't think you'd let me touch you!" he roared back at me.

And he was right.

Or, at least, he *should* have been right.

He's been so hateful that I shouldn't want him anywhere near me.

But I did.

I wanted my best friend back.

"Callum…" I sobbed, as my body shuttered from his confession.

His hand tightened around my neck and I thought he was truly going to end my misery, but his next words had my mind spinning and my body on high alert. "Tell me I'm wrong, Cee," he pleaded. "Tell me you want me to fuck you so hard and deep that it'll take you days to recover, baby."

Even God couldn't have stopped the moan that escaped my lips at his dirty words. They say pregnancy makes a woman extremely horny, but I think I'd want Callum this badly even if I hadn't been pregnant. "Callum, I…"

He ran the hand he had around my throat down my chest and past my stomach until it was resting on my hip. His other hand snaked into my hair and fisted a handful of tresses, yanking my head back in pain and arousal.

My panties were instantly soaked.

His lips started peppering my jaw line as his fingers dug into the flesh of my hip. "Do you want me to beg, Cee? Do you want to hear me say that I want inside your hot, tight pussy so badly, that'll I'll give you anything you want?"

I didn't need him to beg. I just wanted him.

I wanted what we had back.

I just wanted him to care about me like before, but I was too chickenshit to say that. Instead, my hands shot up and fisted in his t-shirt. My legs were giving out on me and I didn't know how much longer I could withstand his assault on my body.

And all the man was doing just planting soft kisses on my face.

I finally responded with the first thing that came to my mind. "Are you just saying that because you don't want to risk being seeing with another woman tonight?"

All the fire, all the heat and all the desperation vanished from his body the second I tacked on the question mark to my sentence. His hands dropped from my body and he stepped back away from me.

I felt cold and so fucking *lonely*.

I missed my best friend so much.

"I thought we cleared that up already, Chloe," he hissed.

I raised my chin, because I was already showing signs of weakness, I didn't want him thinking I was a total pansy. "I want the truth, Callum. What would you do if I truly didn't want to sleep with you again?"

He looked pained at the idea of having a platonic marriage, but I needed words. He has been spewing viciousness at me since the day I told him I was pregnant. I wasn't going to let him believe that he could talk to me anyway he wanted, and then climb into my bed just so he could get his rocks off. "You're saying you would be perfectly fine going the rest of your life without sex, Chloe?"

"No. I guess what I'm asking, is do you think it's possible for us to be a parenting team, but be married in name only? I mean, because if you think it is possible, then maybe we need to not blur the lines and just be parents to this child and nothing more."

One of the hardest things I've ever had to do was hold his gaze as he stalked back towards me. His chocolate orbs were swimming with so many emotions, I couldn't capture even one. "I'll admit, I never should have said what I said to you, but you started it when you made that crack at the reception about sleeping around without the fear of getting pregnant."

"*I* started it?" I squeaked. "What are you...*five?*"

"Do you want to fuck other men or not, Chloe?!" he snapped.

But I countered, "Do you want to fuck other women?"

"No! But make no mistake, Chloe. If you don't spread your legs for me, I will find someone who will." Callum crowded me until my back was up against the wall again. "I am not going to go the rest of my life jacking my dick off just to honor some bullshit wedding vows."

*Bullshit wedding vows?*

I willed my tears to stay locked away and my voice to sound strong. "So, that's the deal, then? Either I sleep with you or I'll just have to make do with you screwing other women?"

He placed his hands on his hips. "And just how long do you think you'll last without sex, Chloe?"

"Apparently longer than you can. But then I'll be busy working and taking care of a baby, so I imagine I'll have my hands pretty full," I snarled at him.

His right hand snaked out and took hold of my jaw. His thumb rubbed back and forth over my skin. His hold was rough, but his caresses were making me break out in goose bumps. "Well, then I suppose since you're able to resist me, but I obviously can't resist you, that makes you the stronger of us two."

"Callum…"

"You want the truth, Cee?" His eyes searched mine. "Well, the truth is that I've been dying to slide back into your pussy since the morning after my graduation party," he murmured.

I gasped.

*Was he serious?*

"So, tell me, Chloe. Do you want me, too, or do you really want a marriage in name only?"

Before I could answer him, the front door swung open almost smashing into me, but luckily, Mya had held onto the doorknob. "Have no fear, I'm…uh…" She shut the door and her head swiveled back and forth between me and Callum as if she was watching a tennis match. "D…do I need…am I interrupting something?"

I pulled my eyes away from Callum. "No, you're not," I said in a voice that I hoped didn't give me away.

I could feel Callum's eye boring into the side of my face. "She's not?"

I turned my head to look at him. "No, she's not. At least, she's not interrupting anything that can't wait," I uttered and instantly regretted it. If we put off this conversation any longer, I was going to lose my mind to confusion.

Because I was so confused.

*So damn confused.*

One minute we're both talking about wanting to sleep with other people and then the next, Callum is confessing to wanting me and *only* me.

And I wanted him, too. But I was too much of a coward to come out and say it because my feelings have been taking a beating from this man for months.

Mya cocked her head at Callum. "What are you doing here, then? I thought you'd be knee deep in dirty pussy and sloppy blow jobs by now."

His hands fisted at his side and his face turned red with fury. What I didn't understand was what exactly he was mad at. He's the one who said he was going to go get his dick wet by someone who wasn't me. And even if he only said it because he didn't think he could have me, he didn't need to beat me in the face with his plans.

Callum faced Mya and his voice was full of disdain and loathing. "You would know all about dirty pussy and sloppy blow jobs, wouldn't you, Mya?"

She smirked. "That's cute. But here is something I do know, Callum. I know how to be a great wing woman, and I know how to offer Chloe my spare bedroom whenever she might need it."

The insinuation that Chloe would let me take random men to her house to fuck wasn't lost on me or Callum. He was in her face in two long strides and I had to jump in between them before my ex-best friend murdered my new best friend. "Callum," I snapped, flattening my hands against his chest in a paltry attempt to hold him back.

I could hear Mya snort behind me, completely unafraid. "Oh, is this like one of those polygamy marriages where the man can fuck all the women he wants, but the wife has to remain faithful?"

Callum peered down at me, ignoring her question, and in a voice as cold as the arctic, he said, "You know what? Fuck who you want, Chloe. I've got better things to do than waste my time trying to keep your legs closed off to the public." And with that, he stormed around us and left, slamming the door behind him. My legs collapsed, and I had to catch myself on the backrest of the sofa.

The second the door shut, Mya shed her armor and her arms wrapped around me. "Oh, God, Chloe. Are you okay?"

I sat against the back of the couch with my hands on either side of me, holding on for dear life. I felt so beaten and exhausted, but I knew…I knew if Mya hadn't shown up, I would have let Callum strip me naked and do whatever he wanted to me. "I'm fine," I whispered unconvincingly.

"Chloe," she sternly disagreed.

I looked into my friend's sweet face and begged for mercy. "Can you just help me out of this contraption and hold me until I cry myself to sleep?" I pleaded.

*Damn pregnancy hormones.*

Her face was immediately flooded with concern. "Oh, honey, of course, I will. But, first, you have to tell me what the hell I walked in on."

I let the tears fall, and I didn't know if they were from exhaustion, emotional abuse and starvation, pregnancy or because this goddamn corset was suffocating me to death.

"Awe, Chloe…" Mya whispered at my tears.

"He told me the only reason he made that comment about sleeping with someone else was because he didn't think I'd give in to him," I divulged to her.

"Uh, I'm sorry. Who did what where?" she asked, clearly confused.

I let out a deep breath and steadied myself for the admission. "He said the only reason he had even entertained the thought of being with another woman was because he wasn't going to go the rest of his life without sex and he didn't think I'd want to be with him."

"Holy shit, Chloe," she breathed out.

"I know." In for an emotional penny, in for an emotional pound, I suppose. "Callum also said he's wanted me since the night we were together.

And then…he kissed me. We kissed."

"Wow." That's it. That's all she had to say.

Before I could comment on her spectacular articulating skills, the front door slammed open so hard, it bounced off the wall and shut back on its own.

Mya and I both jumped off the couch, startled.

*What the hell?*

Callum charged into my apartment like he owned it and he didn't stop until he was standing directly in front of me. He didn't spare Mya a look either as he commanded, "Leave, Mya."

"Hey, wait a sec-" I started, but he wasn't having any of it.

"It's up to you, Cee. I don't give a good goddamn if she stays and watches me fuck you all over this apartment, but you might," he announced straight to my face.

It only took me one second to decide.

"I'll call you later, Mya."

# CHAPTER 6

*Callum*

I had sat in my car cursing all of Heaven for this fucked up situation when I realized I couldn't take it anymore. And now looking down at Chloe, vaguely hearing the front door opening and shutting closed, I knew I made the right decision to come back up here.

I realized we were both struggling and handling this entire ordeal badly. I was saying shit I didn't mean and so was she. We were both hurt and trying to ease our pain by inflicting more pain on the other. It was stupid and cruel.

Chloe looked up at me with lust and hope battling against each other in her deep, blue eyes. She almost cut me off at the knees with her quiet, honest declaration. "Callum, I don't want you to…to…I don't want you with anyone else."

"Awe, baby," I whispered as I took her face in my hands. "I swear to you, I don't want anyone but you, Chloe. But you gotta work with me here, Cee. I feel like not being able to slide inside you is driving me insane." If she was going to be honest, then so was I.

Her dainty hands grabbed at my wrists. "No matter what, promise me there'll be no one else, Callum," she pleaded.

I nodded because it was an easy promise to make to her. I didn't want anyone else. "Chloe, I meant what I said earlier. I'll kill any man who touches you." Again, if we were going to be honest and try to set this fucked up situation right, then I needed to be completely honest with her too.

It took her a few seconds, but she let out a deep breath as if she finally believed me. "Cal-"

I crashed my lips to hers. I didn't want to hear anymore. Every time we opened our mouths, we just succeeded in fucking shit up. It had been a stressful and emotional day and I just wanted to get lost inside her body. I didn't want to keep saying things I was going to regret. I didn't want to hear her tell me things that would keep slicing me open.

Chloe opened her mouth and the second her tongue darted out to fight with mine, I lost it. I tangled my hands in her hair and held on as my lips and tongue assaulted hers. Her hands crawled up in between the cage of my arms and she let out the sweetest moan when they wrapped around my neck and her body was finally flushed with mine.

I pushed against her until the back of the couch stopped our progress and my mind was assailed with image after image of all the filthy fucking things I wanted to do to her.

Real marriage or not, she was my wife by the laws of man and the laws of religion. That meant I owned her. And that meant I could do whatever the fuck I wanted with her body. It belonged to me. All those luscious curves, all those valleys and peaks, all that soft skin…all of it belonged *to me*.

I was going to wreck every inch of her body until I couldn't go on.

I wish now that we had agreed to a honeymoon.

That's another thing I can add to my list of regrets regarding this situation.

I pulled my mouth away and began a trail of wet kisses down her neck. "I'm going to fuck you until you can't take it anymore, Chloe," I whispered against her skin. "I'm not going to stop until you beg me to on your fucking knees."

"Oh, God," she moaned, her head back and eyes closed.

I reached around her back and, one by one, I unhooked each claw on the back of her corset. I wanted her big, full tits out for my mouth by the time I made my way down her neck.

After what felt like a lifetime, my mouth made it to her right nipple just as the corset fell off her body. I couldn't stop the groan that rumbled out of my throat as my hands moved up to cradle each tit in my hand and my mouth closed over her hard nub.

She tasted just as magnificent as I remembered.

Chloe's small, delicate hands got lost in my hair as she held me to her. "*Ohhhhh…*"

My teeth nipped at her peaks and I sucked as much of her tit as I could get into my mouth. I loved her full, round body. I loved how heavy her tits felt in my hands.

As much as it killed me, I pulled away from her-I couldn't stand it any longer. "Take the rest of it all off," I instructed as I started tearing off my clothes.

Her face and chest were flushed in a rosy hue and her tits were being offered up with every shuttered breath she took. "Cal-"

"Take it the fuck off, Chloe, or I swear on all that is holy, I will rip every last scrap from your body," I threatened as I was toeing off my socks. They were the last item of clothing left on my body. I don't think I've ever gotten undress this quickly in all my life.

Chloe must have sensed I was truly on the edge of madness, because she pulled off her stockings, unconcerned with the tearing sounds of the lace, and let her panties follow right after.

*Sweet Christ, she was fucking stunning.*

But I didn't have the control to pamper and ease her into this. Yeah, yeah, yeah…technically, this was her wedding night and she should probably be worshipped and made love to, but it's been months since I've been inside her pussy.

I didn't have enough restraint for making love at this point. My dick was rock hard and ready.

I grabbed her by her arms, flung her over the back of the couch until her ass was up high and presented to me for the taking. Chloe let out a surprised gasp that quickly turned into a moan when I dropped to my knees and ran my tongue in one smooth swipe from her hard clit to her puckered ass.

"Callum…" she rasped out, desperately.

My hands were full of each of her ass cheeks and I had her spread wide and open for whatever I wanted to do to her. "We're not drunk this time around, Cee," I told her. "This time we're going to *know* every fucking feeling."

"God, yes," she moaned back.

I stood up behind her, and without any ceremony whatsoever, I slammed my cock into her hot, wet pussy. She let out a scream at the same time I let out a groan.

I've never had sex without a condom since that night with Chloe, but now that I know what it feels like to be inside her unsheathed, there was no way I'd ever wear one with her now. So, if she didn't want to be pregnant every ten months or so, then she'd better discuss birth control with her doctor soon.

And now being inside her, it hadn't been an illusion. Her cunt felt just as tight and perfect as it did that night that tied me to her for life. I covered her back with my body and said, "And this time I'm going to do what I was too drunk and impatient to do last time, Chloe." I squeezed both her hips in my hands and flexed even deeper into her pussy. "This time I'm going to bury all eight inches of my hard cock into that tight, hot ass of yours." She let out a pant and her pussy tightened around my dick. The idea of taking my cock up her ass was turning her on, and I wanted to praise Jesus.

The problem with last time was we had been beyond drunk. It was the only reason we ended up in bed together. Had we have been sober, it never would have happened. But once the alcohol had worn off in a sea of sweat and moving body parts, we had been so strangled by lust and how good everything felt that we kept going, and going, and fucking going.

When I had awoken to a naked, satiated and passed out Chloe, I had wanted to do it all over again. Well, not the drunk part, but certainly everything else. I had brought her to life with my cock in her pussy and we had one final slow morning screw before she had jumped in her shower and I snuck out while she was in there.

Chloe had been ten kinds of different awkward once we had finished and her scramble to the shower was her avoiding having just cum on my cock. I had wanted to stay and make us an official couple, but having known Chloe for my entire life, I knew she had needed a little space.

What I had never expected was that she'd avoid the hell out of me for the next few weeks while I settled into my new job. And I sure as fuck hadn't expected her finally showing up only to tell me she was fucking pregnant as a result of that night.

Everything up until the moment I walked back into her apartment had been nothing but hate, resentment and cruelty, but that was ending now.

Chloe was my wife, and she was carrying my child and I was done making her pay for ruining my original plans on marrying her.

My fingers dug deeper and deeper into the soft flesh of her hips as I started putting more force behind my thrusts. I wanted to make sure she couldn't get out of bed tomorrow and Chloe's moans were like the best kind of music to my ears. "What do you say, baby?" I coaxed. "Are you going to let me open up that hot ass of yours?"

"Cullen…"

*That wasn't a no.*

It wasn't exactly a yes, but it sure as hell wasn't a no.

I leaned over her back until my chest touched her skin and my lips were at her ear. I never let up on how hard my cock was ramming into her, though. "Have you ever been fucked in the ass, Cee?"

Her cunt contracted, tightening around me like a fist as she moaned, "No…"

I didn't think my cock could get any harder, but hearing Chloe admit that she's never experienced anal sex before had me crazed to be the first to show her. "Well, you will be soon enough, baby."

Her hands turned white knuckled on the back of the couch as she held on. "Oh, God…"

Chloe's surprise and eagerness had me imagining all the things I've ever wanted to do to her. Since the first time my dick's ever gotten hard, Chloe's always been the girl I imagined fucking and ruining with my twisted fantasies.

Even if she never saw me that way, I always saw her in that light and I always knew she'd be my wife. My only real regret was that her virginity had gone to someone else.

But I was more than happy to take the virginity of that other little, sacred hole of hers. A woman letting you fuck her in the ass is a woman so in love with you, the painful intrusion is worth it for her. Or she's so turned on by you, anything you do to her will feel good.

Either was a win for me.

And the dirtier my thoughts ran, the harder I rammed my cock into Chloe's tight pussy. Nothing felt like being inside this woman. I've had my fair share of pussy, but everything about Chloe threatened my sanity. Maybe it was because, with all those other women, I always knew they were temporary- a passing pleasure to kill time and feed my natural urges. I'd never been in a relationship one hundred percent, because I knew I was destined to be with Chloe. Or maybe it was just a simple as the fact that her pussy was hot, tight and made for my cock.

I couldn't help the words that escaped in between the brutal thrusts. "We'll never be that married couple, Chloe," I panted. "We're going to fuck every day. I'm going to spread you wide every fucking day and even when our child is calling you Mom during the day, I'm going to be calling you my dirty slut during the night."

She exploded.

Chloe's orgasm shook her from head to toe and her screams were making my ears ring. It didn't take three thrusts before I was shooting my load deep inside her. The waves wracked my body from the inside out. My wife was cumming all over my cock and it was the best orgasm of my life even though the position was standard.

But I knew it wasn't because of the sex. I knew it wasn't because of the filth I was spewing. It was because this was my first time being inside Chloe as her husband.

Chloe was my fucking wife, and I was never going to fucking let her go no matter how devious her original intentions had been.

I leaned over heaving body and started planting soft kisses along the back of her shoulder. "Christ, Chloe," I muttered, my body relaxed and my brain unguarded. "If being inside your pussy is enough to make me forget this horrible day, I'm pretty sure I'll be able to forget how you trapped me with this pregnancy once I'm inside your tight ass, baby."

I closed my eyes.

I knew I fucked up even before her body stilled underneath me.

Chloe shrugged her shoulder and jackknifed, forcing me to have to pull out and step away from her. I'd done some shitting things to her as of late. And I've said some horrible things to her. And all her varied reactions had run me from cold to hot to confused. But the unsettling, dreadful feeling taking root in the pit of my stomach at the sight of her grabbing the throw blanket off her couch and wrapping it around her body was new.

And foreboding.

When she finished wrapping herself safe, she turned and looked up at me. I expected rage. I expected tears. I expected hurt, confusion, drama...*something*. But I got none of those things.

I got the worst thing in the world.

I got indifference.

I got *emotionless*.

Chloe looked at me with eyes as lifeless as a shark's eyes. "It's been a long day," she said, flatly. "I'm going to head onto bed." Her eyes darted towards the couch and then back up at me. "Make yourself at home if you're going to stay. If not, please lock the door behind you."

"Chlo-"

She clutched the blanket to her chest with one hand while she waved her other one around carelessly. "Don't worry about it, Cee," she said. *She fucking called me Cee.* "Just like I have no plans on spending the rest of my life trying to convince you that I didn't get pregnant on purpose, I'm not going to spend the rest of my life fighting with you. This child doesn't deserve it," she explained. "This kid is innocent even if we're not. Even if you believe *I'm* not."

Chloe walked passed me, leaving me to stand butt naked in her living room without a clue as to how to make this marriage work.

I admit it was a shitty thing to say, but there couldn't be any other explanation for her getting pregnant. Chloe wasn't stupid or irresponsible. If she was, she probably would have gotten pregnant by now if she was just careless.

She knew she wasn't on birth control and she didn't mention it at all. Even if we had gotten carried away the first time, she could have said something before the second, third, fifth time.

The rest of our lives suddenly felt too long.

# CHAPTER 7

*Chloe*

I haven't seen or spoken to Callum since I left him standing naked in my living room Saturday night. Or Sunday morning…whatever.

He was gone when I woke up around noon and I wasn't even sure if he had stayed or gone home. There had been no evidence of him one way or the other.

When I replayed everything from that day/night, what surprises me the most was how I was able to crawl into bed and not cry myself to sleep. Even now, two days later, I still felt rather numb about that night.

When I think of the types of women who would be so low as to get pregnant on purpose to trap a man, I think of low life whores and gold-diggers. I think of women so ugly on the inside they would use an innocent child as a pawn for their selfishness. I think of unfit mothers, resentful fathers and damaged children.

Callum believed me to be in that class of people.

He believed I was the type of woman who would use a child…use *him*. And that hurt.

And it wasn't your average variety of hurt feelings.

Nope. This was much bigger.

I've known Callum all my life. Our parents are best friends. I've sat across from him at a million dinners and countless Thanksgivings. I've opened presents with his family every Christmas since I was born. I've shared all my secrets with this man since I knew what a secret was, and here he was thinking I was…I was trash.

The hurt ran so deep that it turned into numbness. Kind of like when you break a bone, but if you don't see the injury, your mind can convince you it doesn't hurt as bad as it should.

I guess this was my mind's way of protecting my heart. Instead of falling into a dark despair of pain, my mind was numbing me to the pain, allowing me to function.

I sat in my office-much like I did yesterday-not getting anything done. While my emotions were on a tight leash, my mind was still working on the practicalities of my situation.

At this rate, this child was doomed to be raised in a house with no love or affection. His/Her only examples of a healthy marriage will be my parents and Callum's parents. But how much damage will that do to our child to see a real marriage versus what he/she will see at home?

And, God, could I really spend the next twenty years with a man who didn't love me? With a man who couldn't stand the sight of me any more than I could stand the sight of him?

Not to mention all the people we will miss out on meeting because we're trapped in this horrible nightmare. The man who's meant for me might pass me by because I'm too busy trying to survive a loveless marriage.

And what about Callum? The woman of his dreams might move right on by never knowing him because he chose to do the responsible thing.

We didn't deserve this.

I stared down at my hand and the ring sparkling back at me felt like a blade running across my wrists. It was a symbol of nothing but unhappy years to come. It was a symbol of hate, resentment and, eventually, infidelity.

I knew the score. Callum was a gorgeous, virile man. He wasn't going to go the rest of his life without a woman. Hell, he even said as much. He said if I didn't sleep with him, he'd find someone who would.

And I wasn't going to sleep with him again.

I wasn't ignorant to the fact that my body craved his touch. Callum knew how to light my body up and make every nerve sing in pleasure, but my mind and heart outnumbered my body and they knew they wouldn't be able to maintain a sexual relationship with Callum without sorrow, pain and regret following immediately after.

I stared down at my finger and pulled the rings off my finger. I opened my desk drawer, opened my purse and dropped the rings inside the lining pocket. This was a fake marriage. There was no need to have a two-carat diamond platinum ring with a band with equal brilliance. A small, plain gold band would work just as well as that false display of wedded bliss.

"Hey, Chloe." I looked up and saw the handsome face of my co-worker, Benedict Hartman. He was a senior financial analyst, and we'd been working together for about four years.

The man was standing at six foot with a body that fit to match. A group of us would often go out and have drinks at the end of the day, and I always got a small glimpse of Benedict's built when he'd shed the suit jacket, roll up his dress sleeves and relax.

It was a nice glimpse.

He had a head of ebony black hair, a pair of light brown, golden eyes and just looked perfectly male. The man was sporting perfect eyebrows, thick envious lashes around those leonine orbs, high cheekbones, a straight nose, thick full lips and a jawline that made a woman want to pepper with kisses.

He also had a tattoo that peek a little bit beyond his shirt collar, and I'm not going to lie. Many a times I have wanted to see the man without a shirt.

Too fucking bad there was no spark.

If there had been one, I would have been all over that.

Maybe we'd even be married by now with one kid and another on the way. But nope.

No spark. So, I had to just admire him in a purely clinical female appreciative kind of way.

It fucking sucked.

"Hey, Benedict," I greeted back. "What's doin'?"

He walked into my office and took a seat across from my desk. He smiled and said, "I love how you use my full name. No one else does." I just laughed wishing I felt something beyond friendship. "A few of us are making plans for Friday drinks after work," he answered. "You game?"

I hadn't told anyone I was pregnant. Not even mine and Callum's parents knew yet. We were holding off until we couldn't hide it anymore. It wasn't exactly happy news.

The past couple of times my co-workers had gotten together, I had made up excuses not to go, but I knew Benedict would suspect something, eventually. I was never one to bow out of a night of drinking and hanging out. But I also knew if I went and just drank water, they'd all be suspecting something.

And I was a shit liar.

I decided on half-truths to get me through this. "I'm down, just not sure if I'll be drinking though."

His brows rose. "Why not?"

"I went to a wedding this Saturday and…uh, continued way into Sunday morning. I've been a bit of a zombie these past couple of days," I said, hoping my fake laugh didn't sound fake at all.

He angled his head to the side. "Ahhhh. Weddings. They'll do that to you." I smiled. "Who got married?"

"Uh, my best…uh, friend from childhood, Callum," I answered as coolly and as calmly as I could.

"Oh, yeah," he smiled. "I recall you mentioning him a few times." Benedict's eyes widened. "Oh, best friend duties," he deduced. "No wonder you celebrated until the next morning."

"I'm still a little wrecked over it," I grinned, wryly. *The man had no idea.*

He stood up. "Okay, well, water it is," he quipped. "Just as long as your ass is there."

I smiled nodded my confirmation before he strolled out of my office. "Have a good one," I called out.

"You too," he called back.

I felt horrible lying to him, but how do you tell your family and friends that you're now married to a man who hates you because you're pregnant with a child neither of you planned to have with one another?

Worse, how do you explain that your, once, best friend thinks you're nothing but the vile, human female version of a praying mantis without bursting into tears?

But, even if I couldn't drink, maybe an evening out with my co-workers venting about work and talking about anything that wasn't fake marriage related was what I needed.

And maybe if I bought a bunch of rings and slipped them on all my fingers, no one would notice that I was camouflaging a wedding band.

And maybe if I ordered a juice or something instead of water, no one would suspect that I was three months freakin' pregnant.

And maybe, *just maybe,* if The Lord was feeling generous, I hit the lottery this week and be able to live off the money independently for the rest of my life and never have to come in contact with anyone else, thus having to explain my sudden husband and unexpected child.

*But, oh God, how I wanted this baby.*

And not because it was Callum's and I've been stupidly in love with him forever, but because no matter what people's own personal views were, in my eyes and in my heart, I'm a mom right now.

I'm a mom and I'm sitting here with no idea how I'm going to create a happy, secure, love filled home for my child. A happy, secure, love-filled home it deserved. That *every* child deserved. How was I going to be able to create that for him/her?

It wasn't until one of my co-workers popped his head in my door and yelled out bye for the day that I realized I must have thought the past couple of hours away. It was quitting time and I don't think I got one thing accomplished today.

I shut down my computer, grabbed my purse and locked up my office all on autopilot. Even the drive home was on autopilot and it was a wonder I hadn't caused a car wrecked with how spaced out my mind was.

My fogginess was lifted when I entered the lobby of my building to see Mrs. Burks actually trying to maneuver a desk up the stairs. The goddamn elevator has been broken for eons and everyone had to use the stairs, but I still couldn't believe Mrs. Burks was trying to move a freakin' desk up the stairs.

*Fuck the maintenance crew.*

"Mrs. Burks," I hollered. "What on earth are you doing?"

She used her small, 82-year-old, frail body to hold the desk up against the wall when she smiled down at me. "Oh, Chloe, dear. It's so good to see you." Mrs. Burks was the sweetest widow in the world. She was what every grandmother should aspire to be. A 4'11", sharp minded spitfire.

I rushed up to her and placed my hands on the desk, trying to ease the weight off of her body. "What are you doing moving this thing, Mrs. Burks? Why didn't you wait for someone to help you?"

"Oh, child," she cooed. "I've been getting by on my own for years. I still have enough kick in my step to haul this contraption up the stairs."

I didn't want her thinking I was scolding her like a child, so I said, "True. But even the youngest of people are told to use a buddy system when lifting and carrying things if they can."

Mrs. Burks smiled at me. "Well, you're here now," she said. "And you're my buddy, so let's get this done, shall we?"

I laughed. Mrs. Burks was just one of those perfect human beings that you're lucky to know if you ever get the chance. "Let's, ma'am."

I pulled my purse off my shoulder and used the long strap to crisscross it over my torso, and swinging the bulk to rest on my back, I braced myself to help Mrs. Burks lift the desk. "Okay, together now like buddies," she said, chuckling.

It wasn't until I felt all the weight being lifted on my side that I realized she hadn't been lifting it at all. She was scooting it along the steps, completely tearing up the base. At this rate, it would have taken her all week to haul this desk upstairs to her condo.

*Goddamn broken elevator.*

Okay, so it was obvious I needed to get underneath it and take the burden of the weight. I wouldn't be able to live with myself if anything happened to Mrs. Burks. She represented everything that is right in this world, and I did not want her injuring herself for a desk.

"Okay, Mrs. Burks," I began, "we're going to have to double team this thing and I'll take the majority of the weight on this end, while you help guide and steer us on where to go."

Admittedly, when I hear the words double and team together, images of some fantastic porn pops into my head, but you want to know what doesn't pop into my head? The image of an 82-year-old woman giggling and throwing her hands over her mouth to stifle that embarrassed giggle, letting go of the desk and causing it-and me-to meet at the bottom of the stairs.

The giggles ceased and turned into a horrified shriek, *"Chloe!"*

That slow-motion thing? Yeah, that's real.

My mind's clarity was diamond sharp when it recognized the second the weight of the desk hit my chest. It recognized the second my foot began to slip out from under me. Not *slipped* out from under me. But the second it actually started to. My mind was able to pinpoint that one second in time. And even though the entire accident took only about five seconds to happen, time did slow down, and I was able to anticipate the fall onto my back and each tumble down each step.

I was sprawled out on the bottom landing and my mind was able to block out the pain and make me aware enough to throw my arms out to ward off the desk that came hurdling behind me.

I heard the bones in my left arm breaking, but that was quickly ignored as soon as my mind registered the knowledge that I was not going to be able to stop the desk from landing on me. Everything slowed, and I was fully aware of every millisecond it took for my arm to break, the desk to land on top of my body and for the breath to leave my body.

    I was also fully aware of the desk hitting my chest, bouncing over my ribs, hitting my stomach and Mrs. Burks screams in the background.

    Her horrified, shattered screams.

    And those stars?

    The ones you see in cartoons when the toon is hit upside the head? Yeah, those are real too. Everything was real until unconsciousness took over and everything faded to black.

# CHAPTER 8

*Callum*

I hadn't seen Chloe since she shut me out of her bedroom on our wedding night. And so, I was either at Andrew's or the restaurant/bar across from the law office building.

Chloe hadn't attempted to contact me and I hadn't bothered to put in the effort either.

I knew this was my fuck up. I should have left well enough alone, because even if she did get pregnant on purpose, it didn't change the fact that we were married, and we'd be married for life.

I didn't particularly care to be genuinely miserable for the rest of my life and there was no way Chloe and I were going to be able to find a middle ground if I kept throwing her pregnancy back in her face.

She did it. It's done.

The child is here.

The wedding took place.

This was my life.

*Our* life.

"Just tell her already," Andrew said, sitting beside me. "Preferably before you guys kill each other."

I met Andrew our sophomore year at college and became fast friends. He was a couple inches shorter than me, but from all accounts, the guy was a catch. Girls constantly threw themselves at him, but I'd noticed early on that he was selective about who he caught.

Andrew had the whole smart-secretly-tough-guy vibe going on. His hair was a dirty blonde with dark blue eyes. He worked out and kept in shape, and while he was a nice guy underneath it all, Andrew also wouldn't hesitate to throw a punch if it came down to it. Plus, he was stupid smart and working as a structural engineer.

I had called him Sunday evening and shared everything that had gone down at Chloe's, and not because I was a little bitch, but because I was honestly lost as to how to continue with this sham marriage. He had advised me to give her some space, and perhaps give myself a little, too.

"I'm not going to kill her," I said in between drinks of my beer. "At least, not within the next six months."

Andrew snorted. "Look, dude, I get it. I get that you wish this had come about a different way, but you need to quit laying all this at her feet," he stated. "No woman can trap a man if he's being careful and taking responsibility for where he sticks his dick."

"Bullshit," I argued. "You hear about guys getting trapped all the time."

He cocked his head at me and looked at me as if I was the stupidest motherfucker on the planet. "You can curse wicked women to the pits of Hell all you want, Callum, but don't blame them because fucking feels better for us without the condom," he retorted. "If a man buys his own condoms, inspects them himself, puts it on himself, pays attention during intercourse, inspects the condom afterwards, inspects her afterwards…well, then the odds of him getting trapped by an unwanted pregnancy dwindle quite a bit now, don't they?"

Now it was my turn to look at him like he was cracked in the head. "Are you fucking for real?" I asked. "Talk about taking the romance out of it all. If we did that every time we wanted to fuck, the passion would be nonexistent."

Andrew arched a brow. "True," he agreed. "However, there'd never be a question as to whether a pregnancy was a genuine accident or not anymore, now would there?"

I shook my head and tip the beer bottle to my lips. "Look," I said after a drink. "I'm not saying I'm not partly responsible for this pregnancy. All I'm saying is that Chloe should have told me she wasn't on birth control. I trusted her."

"You *say* you're taking responsibility for being neglectful, but you're not *acting* like it," he replied. "In all this time, has Chloe ever blamed you once for not wearing a condom? Has she ever mentioned it, or thrown it in your face?"

The one thing I always advise to my clients is not to squirm; hold still and maintain your composure and confidence. The way you carry yourself can go a long way towards how someone judges you and someone is always judging you. Whether in the courthouse or on the sidewalk.

Well, right now I was doing my best not to squirm in my barstool at Andrew's questions. Even if she's thought it, Chloe hasn't mentioned anything about my failure in this. In all actuality, she's kind of just been taking my shit. She defended herself in the beginning, but she stopped after I made it clear that I didn't believe her and would never believe her.

"No," I finally admitted. "She doesn't make much mention of that night or her pregnancy."

Andrew's sigh almost knocked me over; it was that dramatic. "Callum, if you don't figure out your shit soon, you're going to end up 50 years old and looking back on a miserable life. Or worse, you'll be 30 years old wondering how the fuck you're a divorced, weekend father."

My hands tightened around the beer bottle in my hand.

I could handle looking back on my life when I'm 50 and realizing I lived a miserable existence if Chloe was still with me, having lived miserably right next to me all those years. What I couldn't handle was the second scenario of being divorced and only being able to see my child on the weekends.

Before I could comment, Andrew went on with his advice. "Even without all that crap, how much longer do you think you guys can get away with living separately? Her parents or your parents are bound to visit sooner or later," he pointed out. "You don't think they're going to notice if your spots look *exactly* the fucking same as it did before you guys got married?"

He made an unfortunately damn good point. It made sense for us to live at my place; it was larger. But I knew Chloe no longer felt comfortable there. Besides, her place felt more like a home. My place definitely had that bachelor vibe to it. However, Chloe could kick me out of her house; she couldn't kick me out of mine.

And because I wasn't already feeling like a fucking asshole, Andrew decided to tack on shit I already knew. "And what about her brothers?" he asked, letting out a low whistle. "If they ever find out you married their baby sister because you knocked her up, they're going to tear you to bits."

I turned my head to look at my so-called best friend (now that Chloe hated my guts). "If you're going to flap your yap, can you fill the silence with shit I *don't* know, please?"

I loved Anthony and Stephen Slater, and they were as close to me as my real brother and sister, Timothy and Darlene. But Andrew was right. If they ever got wind of how I was treating their sister, they'd kill me. And while I could take them on separately, together they'd kick my ass, and leave whatever's left for Tim and Leeny.

But all that was based on if I could outrun my father.

See, my mom adored Chloe.

Absolutely *adored* her.

If Gina Rosewood found out the real state of my marriage, she'd lose her shit. And that, in turn, would turn my father into a raving lunatic.

See, where my mother adored Chloe, my father *worshipped* my mother. And we learned early on that if Mom was displeased, Dad became alpha unstable.

Chloe's parents were pretty much the same. Our fathers came from a different era where the woman in your life was the *only* thing that matter. Anthony and Natalie Slater's marriage was the stuff of legends. Where my father worshipped my mother, Anthony Slater *lived* for his wife.

In all the time I've known them, if they were near each other, Anthony was always touching his wife. Natalie could ask him to pick her up some food from any place in the city and Anthony would know exactly what to order for her and how to order it. He knew every detail about his wife and if she ever graces Heaven before he does, I actually fear for his wellbeing.

Come to think of it, I'll probably have to outrun both our fathers at this rate.

I drank the rest of my beer and signaled for the bartender to bring me another one. I didn't give two shits that it was the middle of the week and I had to work tomorrow. I was in the middle of a life crisis here. "I don't know, Andrew," I said. "I don't know if I can ever get past her getting pregnant."

Andrew straightened and looked over at me. "Jesus," he breathed. "Look, Callum, I love you to death, you know that, right?" He didn't let me answer. "But, I swear to God, you have got to be the most egotistical person I've ever met," he said, surprising me. "Do you really think Chloe needs to trap a man into being with her? I mean, fuck, Cal. No disrespect, but your wife is hot as fuck."

*What the fuck?*

"Her face is perfect without any make-up and her body is fucking Hustler centerfold material. An-"

"Andrew, you better watch how the fuck you talk about my wife," I threatened, recalling how he danced with her at our reception. I mean, I knew Andrew wasn't that kind of guy, but he was still a guy. And a guy who had his hands on my wife.

My words didn't faze him at all. "My point being, that if she walked in here right now, every single man in here would look his fill while the brave ones would try to figure out a way to get her home." He turned back to his beer. "I mean, fuck, Callum. You've seen her naked," he added. "Don't tell me you don't know exactly how powerful a punch that woman is packing. Do you really think she needed to get pregnant on purpose to *trap* you? Give me a fucking break."

The bartender chose this moment to drop off my beer. I took a drink and took that moment to let Andrew's words bounce around in my head. "You think I'm being a dick?" I asked.

It seems Andrew's calmed down, because he sighed and said, "I think love has made you stupid." He finished off his whiskey before adding, "I think you were so cemented on your picture-perfect future that you let this mistake-that you *both* made-turn this into something that it's not." He stood up and signaled the bartender to close out his tab. "I think Chloe Slater d-"

"Rosewood," I stupidly corrected him.

He turned and arched a brow at me. "Very well," he mocked. "I think Chloe *Rosewood* doesn't need to trap anyone. I think she's beautiful, smart, witty and sexy as hell. She could have any man she wanted, so why trap the one man she already had? Sex, notwithstanding, she's always had you and she was always going to have you, even if it was just as friends. Why in the hell would she need to stoop to some low level, ratchet ass, gold-digging bitch shit to keep you in her life?" Andrew signed his bill, put his card back in his wallet and turned towards me. "Unless you're telling me the girl you've known all your life really *is* a low level, ratchet ass, gold-digging bitch?"

My jaw clenched, and I'm surprised the beer bottle in my hand didn't shatter from my grip. "You know damn well Chloe is no such thing," I gritted out.

"Then why are you treating her like she is, Callum?" he asked right before he turned his back on me and walked out of the restaurant.

There are certain friends every person needs in their life. You need the person who can make you laugh. They're very important as they are the ones that can keep you from stepping out into oncoming traffic.

Then there's the one who is quiet and humble. They're important because they're the ones who can teach you humility and sensitivity.

You have the angry friend who can put things in perspective when they're overreacting and you're thinking '*hey, shit really isn't that bad*'.

But the one friend every person should have above all others, is the one who isn't afraid of you. The friend who is so confident about your friendship that they are not afraid to tell you when you're being a conceited, self-centered, self-absorbed asshole.

While Chloe had been all the above, Andrew was the latter with touches of all the others. As evident by how he just handed me my ass.

I signaled the bartender again. "Can I get two shots of tequila and another beer, please?"

His blonde brow arched. "That bad?"

I looked up at him and decided that I wanted his unbiased reaction to my predicament. "I got married this weekend to my best friend and girl I've been in love with since I was ten years old. But the only reason we got married is because we had one moment of weakness that resulted in a lifelong responsibility and, now, she believes I only married her because she got knocked up and not before I got a chance to tell her that I've loved her my whole life."

The bartender's brows shot up and he let out a low whistle. "Damn."

"I'm damned, indeed," I agreed.

He cocked his head at me making me think he's heard this one before. He's a bartender; I'm sure there's not much he hasn't heard. "So…since you brought it up, I have a quick question," he said folding his arms over his chest.

"Shoot."

"So, if you've loved her your whole life, I'm guessing you guys have spent many years together as friends and all that." I nodded. "Well, unless you've been an asshole to her all these years, why wouldn't she believe that you love her, even without the pregnancy?" He unfolded his arms and shrugged a shoulder. "Seems to me that if you told her you loved her, she'd have to believe you. Years of your history together would be proof enough, don't you think?"

Here's the thing. You can't get real advice if you don't give the real story.

"I might have accused her of getting pregnant on purpose to trap me," I confessed.

He straightened and cocked his head at me. "I stand corrected, then," he replied. "If your history together isn't proof enough to convince you that she'd never do something like that to you, then your history together isn't proof enough to convince her that you love her." He grimaced in sympathy. "Seems like you guys weren't that great of friends, after all."

He was wrong.

But, unfortunately for me, he was right as well.

And Chloe deserved the biggest apology in all of history.

# CHAPTER 9

*Chloe*

My eyes fluttered open and the burning sensation made me want to just keep them closed forever.

I did my best to sit up slowly because I didn't want to wake Mya. Even though I had told her to go home last night, she didn't. She stayed all evening and night as I cried and cried and cried myself sick.

Since I had made her promise not to tell anyone, she stubbornly insisted that she was not going to leave me alone and would only leave when my parents or Callum finally showed.

I looked over at my friend as she slept on the cot the nursing staff brought out for her. I knew I was going to have to face my parents first thing this morning. I had Mya call my work last night to let them know that I had fallen, broken my arm and was in the hospital. Luckily, all my years of service garnered me sympathies and understanding. My boss told Mya to tell me to take the rest of the week off on sick time and he'd see me on Monday.

I'd never been more grateful for the reprieve.

When I had awoken in the emergency room to be told that I had suffered a severe fall that resulted in a broken left arm, I had immediately panicked and asked about the baby. The looks that played across the faces of the ER doctor and the nurses had told me everything I had needed to know.

I listened unemotionally as the doctor stoically explained how the impact of the desk on my body broke my arm, bruised a couple of ribs and caused me to miscarry. He was very sorry for my loss, though.

There were only four numbers I knew by heart, and those were my mom's, my dad's, Mya's and Callum's. I hadn't been able to get out of the bed, so once I was emotionally stable enough, I had asked the nurse to call Mya for me. Since I had taken off my wedding rings earlier that day, they didn't question if I was married or anything like that. Mya came and stayed and held me through the worst of it. However, I knew I was going to have to send her home and finally call my parents.

I reached over and grabbed a piece of ice out of my hospital water pitcher and threw it at her.

*Bullseye.*

Her body jackknifed, and her head started swiveling around. "Huh? What? Hey? What?"

I don't know how I was able to, but I laughed at her beautiful, bewildered face. "Good morning," I quipped, even though my ribs ached painfully.

I watched as she stretched and yawned herself awake. "Good morning," she greeted back, her voice distorted by the yawns. "How are you feeling, babe?"

"Like a desk fell on me," I replied, dryly.

She didn't comment, but instead, asked, "What's the plan for today? Are they discharging you later?" Mya had called in a sick day at work for me, and I loved her a little bit more for it.

I shrugged. "I don't know. I mean, my arm's casted and I know I'll need to take it easy with my ribs, but I think I need aftercare instructions for…" I couldn't finish.

"Okay," she nodded. "I'll just-"

I stopped her. "You'll just go home and get some rest. I appreciate how you called in for me today, but I can't put it off much longer, Mya. I know I have to tell my parents, especially if I have to stay another night."

She stood up and walked over towards me. I scooted over until she was lying next to me and just one touch was all it took for me to start crying in her arms again.

After a long while, she got up, walked over to the cot and started folding it away. When she was done, she turned back towards me. "Okay, I'm going to go ahead and head out," she said, pain and sorrow clear all over her face. "But you call me the second you need me, you hear?" I nodded, but I was too much of a wreck to respond. Her unconditional love was weakening. It was hard not to fall apart when your family and friends gave you permission to.

Mya walked back over to me, kissed the top of my head, and said, "I love you, crazy girl."

"I love you, too," I sobbed out.

I watched her leave, and it took another visit from the morning nurse and 45 minutes later for me to pick up the phone attached to the hospital bed and dial my mother. It wasn't 30 minutes later, and she and my father were walking through my hospital room door.

My mother immediately rushed the bed and wrapped her arms around my shoulders, careful with my broken arm. "Oh, my God, Chloe, sweetheart! What happened?"

I hadn't explained the accident over the phone. I had just called and told her I was in the hospital and I wasn't sure when I would be released. She didn't wait for an explanation and said she'd be on her way as soon as she grabbed my father.

My father made his way around the bed and caressed the top of my tangled head as I told them about the accident.

"Jesus, Chloe," my father muttered. "You could have been killed."

The word 'killed' ended any sense of composure I had. My eyes started leaking tears and sobs started taking over.

"Oh, honey," my mom cooed. "It's okay. You're fine," she said with glossy eyes. "Everything will be fine. It's just a broken arm."

"Bu…but…it's…it's n…not jus…just a bro…ken arm, Mo…m," I cried.

Even through my sobs and pain, I could feel my father stiffen next to me. "What do you mean, Chloe? And, now that I think about it, where the hell's Callum?"

It took an entire five minutes before I could gather myself together and confess everything. They stood by silently as I told them the whole story between sniffles, cries and bouts of rib pings and pains. I told them how I've always loved Callum. I told them about the night of his graduation party. I told them about how I got pregnant. I told them how Callum refused to let this come between them and his parents. I told them how he accused me of trapping him and I told them how much I hated him for thinking so low of me. I told them how we weren't living together. And I even told them how we discussed the possibility of marriage in name only.

The only thing I spared them were the details of our sexapades and the venom of our arguments. I knew they were going to be disappointed, but I didn't want them hating Callum. Because, through it all, I didn't hate him. Unfortunately for me, I still had too much love for him than was wise.

I sat silently as my father walked around my bed to stand next to my mother. I closed my eyes because I knew it was going to be all bad now. He was standing next to her in a stance of a united front, only I didn't know if it was a 'we're here for you' stance or a 'you're dead to us' stance.

When I couldn't stand their scrutiny any longer, I pleaded with them. "Can you guys say something, please?"

My mother darted her eye towards my dad and cleared her throat before returning her brown gaze back my way. "It's a lot to absorb, Chloe," she stated simply.

My father's blue eyes-the very ones that matched mine-were filled with so much weight, it was hard to look at him. "Dad?"

He didn't respond right away. I knew my dad, and I knew he was trying to find a way to reprimand me without adding more hurt to my already battered emotions. He was disappointed and probably pissed off as hell but, unless it came to my mother, if us kids got into a bind, he always did his best to put his parental responsibility above his emotions of anger or disappointment. It was only when we upset our mother that he didn't care about parental responsibility and would let his wrath loose on us.

My father loved my mother in a way that you only read about in romance novels.

"I'm just having a hard time understanding why you and Callum would believe that your…indiscretion would cause a riff, between us and the Rosewoods, Chloe," he finally said. "You and Callum are grown adults. I feel confident in saying that we all would have let you guys figure it out like adults had we known the truth."

"I don't know, Dad," I admitted. "I think, maybe, Callum and I were just in such emotional shock we weren't exactly thinking straight. We panicked."

"That's why you insisted on paying for the wedding yourselves, isn't it?" my mother asked.

I nodded. "I couldn't stomach the idea of you guys wasting your hard-earned money on a fake wedding. I was already struggling with the lies as it was."

And, then, my father showed me, once again, why he was my hero. "Well, all that's over. What's done is done, and no matter how we feel about it, we can't go back and change any of it." He reached over and took my mom's hand in his left one and rubbed my leg with the other. "What matters now is your loss and how you feel now, Chloe. What do you need from us, honey?"

And just like that, I started bawling all over again. I dropped my head in my hands and cried through the pain of my bruised ribs and sore shoulder. My arm was in a sling, but still mobile. And to my parents' credit, they didn't try to placate me with soothing words or false reassurances. They just me cry out my pain and let me grieve how I needed.

When I could finally get it together again, I answered him honestly. "This entire ordeal has been nothing but pain and heartache since that…night, Dad. I just want it to all go away. I want you guys to still be best friends with the Rosewoods and not to hate Callum when he was just as confused as I've been. We messed up, but that's where I want the unhappiness to end."

My father just gave me one solemn nod, while my mother went on to ask the tough questions. "So, what does this mean for you and Callum now that…? What do you see happening now, Chloe?"

I reached over to the cheap tissue box that was sitting on my hospital tray and pulled out a shitload of tissues. I cleaned my face, and after taking a sip of water from the little plastic complimentary cup, I answered her honestly, as well. "I imagine we'll be getting a divorce, and hopefully with some time, we can put this behind us and find a way to remain friends of some sort."

My parents exchanged a look that I couldn't decipher, but to be fair, I was an emotional wreck. I couldn't concentrate on anything long enough to crack any mystery codes.

"Chl…Chloe, honey," my mom began, "are you sure you want to make permanent decisions like divorce, right now, while you're under so much emotional stress?"

The sigh I gave felt like it came from my soul. "Mom, Callum only married me because I got pregnant," I reminded her. "Now that I'm…no…no longer pregnant, I'd say divorce is a sure thing."

Before she could argue, my father jumped in. "Does Callum even know, Chloe?"

I shook my head. "No," I whispered. "I called Mya when I found out and she stayed with me until I kicked her out this morning. I called you guys next. Uhm…I'm going to call Callum after you guys leave and tell him. I'm also going to encourage he tell his parents so that this doesn't put you guys in an uncomfortable position."

"Don't worry about us, Chloe," my mom chided. "The Rosewoods and us will be fine. Just worry about getting better, honey."

I looked at my parents and the shame I was feeling went way beyond the usual guilt of letting my parents down. "I'm so sorry, Da-"

He held his hand up to stop my apology. "Chloe, we know you're sorry," he said. "And as disappointed as we are that you didn't trust us enough with this, your mother is right. Right now, you just need to worry about healing and moving on from this. You have more than just physical injuries to contend with at the moment. Just get better, sweetie."

They stayed all morning until the doctor made his rounds and informed me that they wanted to keep me over for one more night before sending me home. He wanted me to speak with a counselor before heading home, and unfortunately, she had been called away for a patient emergency. Physically, he was confident that I'd made a full recovery and there'd be no long-lasting effects.

And because I was exhausted…

Or a coward…

I waited until late afternoon to call Callum. We hadn't spoken in days, and while I could have had Mya pull out my phone from my purse and bring it to me to check, I didn't. I didn't want to see how Callum *hasn't* called me in days.

He answered on the second ring. "Chloe?" It took everything I had not to burst into tears and fall apart when I heard him pull the phone away and tell someone, "Sorry, but I have to take this. It's my wife."

"Cal…" I took a deep breath and tried to steady my voice. "Callum?"

"Yeah?" He sounded preoccupied but focused on me.

"I…just call…called to let you know that…uhm, I'm in the hospital. I-"

"What?!" he barked over the phone. "What the fuck do you mean you're in the hospital? What the fuck happened?"

"Cal-"

"What happened, Chloe?" he interrupted. "Are you okay?"

"I fell yesterday and-"

His voice went from concerned emotion to coldly lethal. "Yesterday?" he interrupted again. "You've been in the hospital since fucking yesterday and you're barely calling me *now?*"

My chest caved and the pinch in my heart felt real. This is the same man who threatened to murder me on our wedding day because I was a low life gold-digger. He had no right to feel offended because I waited to call him. He should be thankful that I was calling him at all. This was a courtesy call. It's not like I really expected anything more from him.

And, then, suddenly, I didn't know if it was the stress of the past three months. I didn't know if it was the emotional turmoil from losing my baby. I didn't know if it was the shame from confessing to my parents. Whatever it was, I didn't want to be the only one hurting and Callum deserved to be my target. "I only called because we need to talk and-"

"Where are you?" he asked, his voice colder than before.

"Mass General," I answered, politely. "If you-" I didn't get a chance to finish.

He'd hung up on me.

# CHAPTER 10

*Callum*

She's been in the hospital since yesterday and she didn't bother to call and let me know. Hell, she could have sent a fucking text. Something. *Anything.* But no, she only called me because she thinks we need to talk.

I knew things were shit between us right now, but I had no idea we'd fallen so far that Chloe would think that I wouldn't care that she was in the hospital. Over 25 years of friendship and she didn't think I'd care that something had happened to her.

Last night I spend all night replaying Andrew's words in my head only to realize that he was right.

The bartender was right, too.

I was so focused on this pregnancy ruining my perfect proposal plans, that I let it ruin everything else.

And, guilt, it was a motherfucker alright. I let my anger ruin our courtship, our wedding, our wedding night and everything in between.

The only good thing to happen today was that her phone call came in between court appearances. I had just finished pissing off the D.A. by pointing out their incompetency and informed them that this was the last continuance I would allow. According to the laws of the land, defendants had a right to a fair and speedy trial and this case was becoming anything but speedy.

The goddamn cop who pulled my client over and supposedly found drugs in his car was also the same cop who was fucking my client's wife. Now, that wouldn't be a problem had the officer stepped back and let his partner handle the traffic violation, but he hadn't. He supposedly pulled my client over for not coming to a complete stop and, for whatever reason, the simple ticket issue turned into a search of my client's car and finding drugs.

First, my client didn't do drugs. And even if he did, he wouldn't be stupid enough to not come to a complete stop if he knew he had drugs in the car. If he was that stupid, then he deserved to go to jail.

The prosecution was having problems with collaborating witness statements-primarily the two officers who pulled my client over. I had every intention of beating this case and then filing a civil liberties case against the city.

I hated dirty cops.

My next court appearance was supposed to be an arraignment against another client for embezzlement and that case was weak as fuck, as well. I had no doubt my paralegal assistant could handle the arraignment. It was nothing but pleading not guilty and setting another court date.

I dialed Chelsea's number and gave her a rundown of what's to be expected as I opened my car door, threw my briefcase on the passenger seat and got in. I also told her to cancel the rest of my day. I wasn't sure what to expect once I got to the hospital, but I'd rather have my day cancelled to deal with whatever awaiting me.

I also wasn't too proud of the kick in my chest when Chelsea exclaimed 'your *wife*' over the phone. I didn't spend the day hiding my hand, but I hadn't exactly gone out of my way to share my wedding news with anyone, either.

The more I thought about things, the more I realized I should just call Andrew over and have him kick my ass. Or call Chloe's brothers and have them really do a number on me. I've been nothing but a fucking asshole to her for the past two months and her being in the hospital without even a thought to call me was a real fucking eye opener.

I synced my phone and dialed Andrew before I pulled off into traffic. He answered on the third ring. "What's up? You still being a snatch napkin?"

*Snatch napkin?*

Jesus, where did this guy come up with shit like that?

"I'm actually on my way to the hospital," I answered, ignoring his question of being a snatch napkin.

His voice instantly changed. "Are you okay?"

I hit a red light and irritation took over. I needed to get to Chloe. "Chloe just called me telling me she's at Mass General."

"Why?" he asked on full alert. "Is she okay?"

"I think so. I don't know." God, it actually hurt to say those words. My wife was in the hospital and I had no idea what was wrong with her. Andrew was right. I am an egotistical jackass.

"What the fuck do you mean, you don't know?" he barked. "How in the fuck don't you know, Callum? She's your fucking *wife*."

The light turned green, and I gunned the engine harder than I should have. Andrew's glaring observations were pissing me off. Not at him, though. This fuck up was all me. "I know that," I snapped. "She called and said she's been in the hospital since yesterday and said we needed to talk." Andrew silence was so deafening, I had to check the screen to check if we were still connected. "Andrew?"

The clearing of his throat came over the speaker. "Uhm...she's been in the hospital since yesterday, Cal?"

I let out a frustrated sigh. The traffic was fucked, and I was an asshole. "Yeah, man," I confirmed. "She's been there since yesterday and she barely called me a few minutes ago."

"Because she said you guys needed to talk?" he asked, his tone hesitant.

"Well, yeah," I replied. "I'm guessing there's probably some issue with insurance or something."

And then Andrew hit me with something that had never occurred to me. "Callum, what if...if something's wrong with the baby?"

My foot on the brake almost caused a wreck.

Cars were honking all around me and it took me a second to realize I better pull off to the side of the road. I put my foot back on the gas pedal and managed to coast my way onto a side street and park along the curb without killing anyone.

"Callum?"

My hands tightened on the steering wheel and it was all I could do to breathe. "No," I denied. "She would have told me if something like that was wrong, And."

"May...maybe she didn't want to tell you something like that over the phone, Cal."

"No," I denied, again. "There's no way something's wrong with the baby, Andrew. She called because of insurance or something like that. If she was that seriously hurt, she wouldn't have waited an entire day later to call and tell me." I heard the words coming out of my mouth, but I wasn't entirely convinced.

"Are you sure about that, Callum?" he asked. I knew he wasn't asking to be a jerk, but the question was enough to put me on the defensive.

"Of course, I'm fucking sure!" I spat. "If she was injured enough to cause a goddamn miscarriage, she would have called me. She would have needed me there!"

He remained silent, and that silence scared me enough to fear wondering just how much I've fucked thing up with Chloe. But...

Surely, if she had lost the baby, she would have called me. I mean, there's no way she would go through something like that alone. *Would she?*

"Look, Callum," Andrew replied, his voice calm and firm as if he's trying to keep me from losing my shit. Hell, maybe he is. "I just want you to be prepared in case...well, in case it's worst case, ya know?"

"Why..." Jesus, I was a mess. "Why would she wait a day to tell me if it was...worst case? That's not something a woman needs to go through alone."

There was a clipped silence right before Andrew pointed out, "She wouldn't have been alone, Cal. I'm pretty positive Mya's been at her side this whole time."

The laugh that left me was hollow and weak.

Of course.

Mya.

*Her new best friend.*

The person she no longer needed me for because she had Mya Fucking Carlson to be her best friend.

"Callum, I hate to do this to you, because I know your mind is probably your worst enemy right now," Andrew said through the speaker. "But you have to prepare yourself for the worst and that includes the possibility that Chloe may ask for a divorce if…if…you know."

*Jesus Fucking Christ!* First, I might be losing my baby and now I might be losing my wife???

"I gotta go, And," I said cutting off anything else he might have wanted to say. One thing I knew for sure was that Chloe was hurt. That's what I needed to focus on and get to the hospital and see what all I was dealing with before going all Chicken Little.

I hung up and pulled my car back onto the road, but Andrew's concerns were still banging loudly around in my head. I didn't want to think about the possibility that we lost the baby, but as long as Chloe was okay, we could still have a boatload of more kids. Of course, nothing could replace this baby because this baby was special.

*Our first.*

And that's when it hit me. It didn't matter how this baby came to be, he/she was ours. It was the best pieces of Chloe and the best pieces of me crafted together.

*God, I don't think I've ever felt this big of a fool.*

A million hours later, I finally pulled into the hospital parking lot. I parked in the first empty spot I saw and jogged my way to the entrance.

When I got to the visitor's counter, the admittance clerk was on the phone. I did my best to wait patiently, when what I really wanted to do was rip the goddamn phone from her ear and demand she tell me where Chloe was.

An eternity later, she finally addressed me. "Hello, Sir. How may I help you?"

"Chloe Rosewood, please."

She looked down at her computer screen and started tapping away at her keyboard. "I'm sorry. We don't have a Chloe Rosewood in admittance. Are you sure you're at the right place?"

Worry quickly gave way to anger. Once I knew she was one hundred percent okay, I was going to strangle the fuck out of her. I cleared my throat and did my best to sound civil. "How about a Chloe Slater?"

Nancy-her nametag read-went back to tapping away at her keyboard, and a few seconds later, smiled up at me. "Oh, yes," she replied. "We do have a Chloe Slater." I gritted my teeth as she pulled out a visitor's sticker and wrote down Chloe's room number on it. "Here you go, Sir. Room 3116."

I snatched the visitor's sticker out of her hand and half-ass ran towards the elevators. I stood there waiting for the elevator seething at her blatant refusal to acknowledge our marriage.

Chloe was a goddamn Rosewood now, and after today, she was going to start acting like one. I had a quick, irrational thought of strapping her down and tattooing my fucking name across her chest, that way she would no longer be confused.

The elevator dinged, and the doors swooshed open. Thank God it was empty. I was liable to lose my shit if I had to make a million stops in between floors. I stepped into the elevator and pushed the third-floor button, stood back, watched the doors closed and told myself to fucking breathe.

What if Andrew was right?

I had no idea what I would do if she lost our baby.

None.

But what I did know was that…if the worst did come to pass, we'd get through it together. We'd get through this together and I would get my best friend back. Contrary to Andrew's opinion, I wasn't so egotistical to think I could undo everything that's happened, but I was determined to make things better moving forward.

I owed Chloe the biggest of apologies. I just prayed she can forgive me.

The elevator came to a stop, and the doors opened, giving me access to the hospital's third floor. I found the floor's nurses' station and approached, hating the words that were going to come out of my mouth. "Hello," I greeted as politely as I could. "Room 3116. Chloe Slater."

The pretty, brunette nurse smiled at me before tapping away at her keyboard, very much like the downstairs receptionist. "Oh, okay," she said, smiling back up at me. "If you just go down this hallway, around the second corner, she'll be the second room on your left."

"Okay," I said as I gave her a quick nod.

"Just follow the signs if you get turned around," she advised as I was already walking away from the counter.

It only took me a minute to find Chloe's room, but I didn't go in right away. I knew I needed to pull my shit together before going into her room. I had to erase my mind of all of Andrew's doomsday predictions and listen to what she had to say. I had to make sure she was okay and then I had to make sure the baby was alright.

I didn't want to bully her, but I also had to let her know that she'd be going to my place once they released her. There was no way I was going to let her go back to her apartment to take care of herself alone. It didn't matter that she had Mya or her parents or brothers.

Chloe was my wife, and even though I've done a shit job of it so far, it was my job to take care of her and I was going to start now.

I took a deep breath and put my hand on the doorknob praying against all prayers she and our baby were fine.

The alternative was unacceptable.

Too bad it took something like this for me to realize how important the family I had was.

# CHAPTER 11

*Chloe*

In the fastest-or slowest-30 minutes known to man (depending on your perception), Callum was walking through the door to my hospital room. He looked like he just came from court, but hell, I didn't know anything about his days, so maybe he did. Tears threatened as I took in how beautiful he looked.

He stopped when he stood next to my bed and, if shit wasn't fucked up before, things really got uncomfortable when he reached over to caress my face and I flinched and moved back. His hand curled into a fist as he dropped it to his side.

I kept my head down as he finally asked, "So, what happened?"

My hands played with the loose threads of the hospital blanket and I focused on those little loose threads as I recapped what happened. "I'm not sure if you know my neighbor Mrs. Burks, but she's 82 years old and the sweetest woman." I had to swallow before I went on. For some reason, it felt as if I had done something wrong, but that could just be my own self-guilt over losing my baby. "She was trying to move a desk up the stairs on her own, because the ele-"

"The elevator doesn't work," he interrupted in. "Yeah, I know."

I cleared my throat. "Anyway, I was helping her move it when she…lost her grip and…" I took a deep breath. "Long story short, I fell, and the desk fell with me." I lifted my arm the best I could to show him the cast, even though I'm sure he noticed it as soon as he walked in the room.

"Did you land on your arm?" he asked, quietly.

"Uhm, no. I…uhm, landed on my back. I broke my arm…" I finally looked up at him. "I broke my arm trying to hold off the desk from falling on me."

His deep brown eyes searched mine as he asked, "The desk fell *on* you?"

"Yeah," I answered. "My arm didn't do much in the way of preventing it." It was a lame attempt at a joke, and it fell flat. *Flat, flat.*

"And the rest of you?" His hands were still balled up into fists at his side as he asked.

"I have a couple of bruised ribs and just a lot of aches and...pains," I answered, evading his real question.

Callum grabbed the bed rail until his knuckles were bloodless. "And the baby?"

I didn't possess the strength to voice the harsh truth. My eyes started brimming over and I gave my head a tiny shake letting him know without having to actually say the words.

I didn't want to say the words.

In my heart it was real, but I wasn't ready to share my pain with Callum. Sharing it with Mya and my parents was different. They loved me unconditionally, and I knew they would only hurt for me and not blame me.

I watched, silently, as Callum's hands let go of the railing and his body fell into one of the chairs sitting next to the bed. He dropped his head in his hands and the room went completely still. Except for the beeps and bops from the machinery, the room had no life.

Five seconds later, a Callum I'd never met before made an appearance as he stood up, and grabbing the hospital tray, threw it across the room *"Why in the fuck would you try to move a fucking desk knowing you're pregnant?!"* he screamed over the clattering of the tray's contents against the wall.

"Callum-"

He grabbed the railing and, as he pulled and pushed against it, I wondered if he wished it was my neck. "Tell me, Chloe," he yelled. "Did you take off your wedding rings before or after your fucking accident?!"

My eyes widened, and my head swung back and forth.

*No!*

*No, no, no.*

I knew he thought the worst of me because he believed I got pregnant on purpose, but he couldn't think…

*No.*

Callum *could not* believe I'd hurt myself on purpose to…to…

My stomach heaved at the very idea that he might believe I'd purposely do something to lose my baby. If I hadn't wanted my child, I would have gotten an abortion as soon as I found I was pregnant and would have never told him about it. I destroyed our lives because I wanted my baby. How could he think otherwise?

"No, Callum," I shouted, horrified. "The rings have nothing to do with what happened."

"Tell me!" he kept screaming.

"I took them off at work," I screamed back. "They're in my purse."

He stormed back towards the bed until he was towering over me. I'd never see him so mad. And I'd never seen him direct so much hate my way. Not even on our wedding day. If I had any reservations about if Callum really hated me or not, I didn't have them any longer.

Before he could say anything-or kill me with his bare hands-a nurse entered the room looking flustered and alarmed. "Ms. Slater-"

Callum whipped around and turned all that focused fury on the poor nurse. "Her fucking name is *not* Slater," he spat. "It's Rosewood. Her name is Chloe Fucking Rosewood! *Mrs.!*"

The nurse looked shocked and stricken, and we both watch in shocking fright as Callum walked over to the wall, pull my purse off the coat hanger and tear it apart until he found the rings.

I could only stare wide eyed and confused as he grabbed my broken arm and shoved the rings back on my finger. "Sir!" the nurse objected when she saw him grab my arm. "I'm going to have to ask you to leave right this minute!"

My knuckle was bleeding from where he forced the rings back on. My cast reached my knuckles, but I could still move my fingers. My arm was what was actually broken, not my hand.

Callum ignored the nurse and leaned down into my face. "The only reason I'm going to walk out of this room is because I'm not going to ruin my career by getting arrested," he explained. "But make no mistake, Chloe," he seethed. "There's no way in hell this is over. Jesus. Fuck!"

I had to tell him the complete truth. He had to know he was free. "I...my parents...Callum, I told them everything," I confessed. "We don't have to stay marr-"

He threw his head back and his laugh was cold and cruel. When he looked back down at me, he said. "You think I give a fuck if your parents know why we got married? Do you think I give a fuck about *my* parents? Our friends? *Anyone else but you?*"

He was starting to sound unhinged and I think the only reason the nurse hadn't called security yet was because she was curious to see how this was going to play out. She was enthralled with our little drama.

I didn't give thought to my next words, but no matter how insensitive they might have been, they were still the cold, hard truth. "You're not trapped anymore, Cee."

He stepped back as if I had slapped him. But then his face went from rage, to shock, to a mask so cold, my body broke out in shivers. A heartbeat of silence passed before he said, "Baby or no baby, Chloe, over my dead body will I let you divorce me." I gasped at his seriousness. "I don't give a fuck what you want or how you feel about our marriage, I am *never* going to let you divorce me." He turned and walked out before I could say anything.

When the door shut, the nurse rushed to my side. "Oh, my God! Are you okay, honey?" she asked as her hands ran over my body looking for signs of distress.

"I'm fine," I assured her. I looked over at the mess Callum made. "I'm so sorry about the mess. I can clean it-"

"No," she said, firmly. "Stop it." She looked around the room and said, "It's nothing that can't be cleaned up in a jiffy." It was odd that the only thing I could think of was that she wasn't old enough to be saying words like 'jiffy'.

*Oh, God. I must be losing my mind.*

I watched helplessly as she started picking up the items Callum threw from my purse. I looked down at my rings and I couldn't find the strength to wipe the blood off my finger.

It just didn't make any sense. Why would he want to stay married? Granted, he was probably just emotional and not thinking straight, but he did say 'baby or no baby' and that was giving me cause for concern.

There was no way Callum and I could stay married after something like this. Not only did he accuse me of getting pregnant on purpose, he actually accused me of acting reckless to purposely lose our baby. And it seemed with every passing day, the hurt cut deeper until nothing was capable of stopping the bleeding.

From below the bed, the nurse said, "My name's Sheryl, by the way, and I'll be your afternoon nurse."

God, I bet she was wishing she wasn't. "Hi, Sheryl, I'm Chloe and, again, I'm so, so sorry for everything. I can-"

"Shush your mouth, child." *Child?* She looked like she was younger than me, yet she was speaking like an 80-year-old southern grandmother. "There's nothing to be sorry about," she said, picking up the mess from the tray. "Men…well, they're men," she stated as if that said it all.

"Do you mind me asking how old you are?" I needed to know.

Sheryl stood up with the pitcher in her hands and smiled at me. She was very pretty, with shiny blonde hair, big cornflower blue eyes, and the sweetest face. She looked like a doll. "I'm 23," she answered.

I smiled back. "You don't talk like a 23-year-old," I replied, letting on why I asked.

She let out a small chuckle. "That's because I was raised by my grandmother," she divulged. "I'm originally from Louisiana but moved to California to get my nursing degree."

"Oh, that explains a lot," I said, smiling.

"I know," she grinned. "You're not the first person to take notice that I talk like an 80-year-old grandmother with too much time on her hands."

I dropped my head back, closed my eyes and let out a sigh. I was feeling so much; I didn't know where to even begin to sort my feelings out. I decided to stick with simple. "Well, it's nice to meet you, Sheryl."

I could still hear her moving around when she replied, "It's nice to meet you, too, Chloe. Although, it would have been nicer to meet you under different circumstances."

"Yeah, sorry about Callum," I apologized again.

"No, not him," she corrected. "I meant your accident. I'm sorry for your loss, honey."

Tears silently started leaking down the sides of my face. I couldn't help how devastated I felt. It didn't matter that I had only been three months pregnant. From the moment I found out I was pregnant, I was in love like only a mother could be. "Thank you," I whispered as I opened my eyes.

Sheryl came and stood over my bed and looked all of her 23 years, but her words sounded like they were coming from someone who's lived too many years to count. "I know I don't know you…an…and you don't know me," she started. "But…I feel as if you need some…comfort from someone on the outside looking in." My eyes started silently leaking again. "Family…well, family has too much of itself invested in you. They've known you your entire life, so they genuinely believe they're experts at what you need, because they know you so well." She pursed her lips. "The problem with that, is that no one really knows the real you. Even family," she pointed out.

"They mean well," I said, defending families everywhere.

She smiled. "Oh, of course, they do. I'm not saying they don't. What I'm saying is that friends and family advice is often skewed because of their feelings for you. But what they rarely realize is that you don't need advice. You're a grown woman who can make her own decisions. You don't need anyone to tell you what to do *unless* you ask for that advice."

I wiped my face and Sheryl handed me a tissue for my nose. After a few seconds, I asked, "So, what's your…observation about Callum and what happened earlier?" I don't know why I was asking a perfect stranger, but she was right about my family and friends. They'd never be able to give me unbiased advice.

Sheryl reached out and grabbed my hand. "That man is pissed," she said straightforwardly, causing me to laugh. She smiled. "I don't know anything about what is going on between you, but no man gets that angry if he doesn't care."

I decided to give her the Cliff's Notes of our marriage. "We used to be best friends, then we slept together one night, and that resulted in me getting pregnant. Our parents are friends and so he insisted on getting married because he didn't want to ruin their 30-year friendship." I let out a sigh. "And now he thinks I purposely put myself in danger to lose the baby."

Sheryl cocked her head at me and, after a few agonizing seconds, said, "Honey, no man ties himself to a woman for life just to secure his parents' 30-year friendship." I started shaking my head, but she stopped me. "Just hear me out, Chloe," she insisted. "Your parents have been friends for over 30 *years*. You think their *grown* children getting pregnant would have ruined that? If anything, it would have made things easier. That man is mad at you for something, but it's not because you got pregnant. And maybe he just isn't sure why he's mad yet and that's what he's holding on to."

"Whatever his reasons, they don't excuse his behavior," I argued.

"No, they don't," she agreed. "But you guys cannot solve this argument if you don't even know what it is you're fighting about." She squeezed my hand.

"Fight to keep him, fight to leave him…but just *fight*."

I broke down in tears and Sheryl didn't leave me until I faded into slumber.

## CHAPTER 12

*Callum*

I sat at my parents' kitchen table with my head in my hands. The only small consolation I had was that I had updated my will when Chloe had told me she was pregnant, so everything was in order, for when after my parents killed me.

When I had stormed out of Chloe's hospital room, I lost all sense of surroundings until I found myself sitting in the reception area an hour later regretting how I reacted.

I had gone up there with every intention of making things right between us, but the second she told me about the baby, I lost it.

When I first walked in and took inventory of her person, the casted arm, the scrapes…all of it had faded away when I noticed she didn't have her wedding rings on. Granted, there could have been a perfectly acceptable injury or hospital reason for them to have been removed, especially with it being her left arm that was broken, but that's not what I saw.

I saw her registered as Chloe Slater. I saw her without her rings on. I saw her battered and broken without a husband at her side.

*Because. She. Didn't. Fucking. Call. Me.*

I saw her acting single and trying to take care of herself. And all my fuck-ups, all my regret erupted like a goddamn volcano when she looked at me with those quiet tears in her eyes, still trying to handle shit on her own, as she confirmed Andrew's worst prophecy.

And, God, when she said I wasn't trapped anymore like that was a good thing, I'd never felt such rage in all my life. Then fear at her implications.

She also called me Cee, and that was my undoing.

"Okay, okay," my mother murmured, all aflutter as she and my father walked into the kitchen and sat down across from me. "We're here. We're here. What's the emergency, Callum?"

When I arrived at my parents, I found my mom in the kitchen and I insisted she go grab my dad from the backyard. I wasn't about to run through this twice. It was bad enough I had to leave here to go speak with Chloe's parents afterwards; I wanted to rip the band aid off this one.

"Uhm, have you guys spoken to The Slaters lately?" I only asked because I wanted to know how much my parents knew or if they were truly clueless.

"I spoke with Natalie yesterday, but...well, we haven't spoken today," my mother answered looking over at my dad.

"I haven't spoken to Anthony in a couple of days," he said. "Why?"

"Oh, my God," my mother exclaimed. "Are they okay? The kids?"

"No, no, no, Mom," I hurried. "The Slaters are fine. A.J. and Stephen are okay too. Well, as far as I know."

My mother's eyes instantly watered. "And Chloe?" she whispered.

"Chloe's alright, right, son?" my dad asked sternly. Like I said, he was a firm believer that a man's sole purpose on earth was to take care of his woman.

*Fuck!*

I looked at both my parents and prayed for mercy. "Before you yell at me, kick my ass or disown me, I just need you guys to hear me out, okay?"

My mother's face looked wary and my father leaned back in his chair, crossing his arms over his chest. He already looked pissed. "Okay," he agreed even though I knew he was already thinking up ways to dismember me.

I let out a deep breath and started at the beginning, telling them everything; every insensitive, hurtful, vile thing I've done to Chloe since the night of my graduation party.

And, yep.

It pretty much went the way I figured it would, with my father exploding and my mother in disappointed tears.

*"What?!"* my father roared across the table as he stood up and braced his hands flat on the table's surface. I'm guessing it was the table or my throat.

"Dad-"

He pointed a finger at me. "Don't Dad me, Callum Rosewood! How could you even..." he sputtered, not even able to finish his sentence.

"Callum, honey," my mom jumped in, "we just don't understand *why*."

I didn't hesitate. I jumped right in on trying to explain the why part of my assholery. My father had sat back down by the time I was done explaining everything that was wrong with me. "Look, I know-"

"Gina, can you give me and Callum a few moments, please," my father asked of her, interrupting what I was about to say.

*Fuck.*

He was going to kill me, and he didn't want to upset my mother by making her watch.

I looked over at my mother as she just nodded and, rising out of her chair, left me alone with my father. The fact that she left me alone with him knowing he was probably going to kill me spoke volumes of just how disappointed she was in me. I was her youngest for crying out loud. Her *baby*. Yet, she was so disappointed in me; she was okay with my impending murder.

"Dad-"

He held his hand up to stop me from talking. He crossed his forearms and leaned on the table, his gaze never wavering. His words hit me like a freight train, and I wished he had gone with killing me instead. "Son, maybe you need to let this divorce go through if that's what Chloe wants. You-"

This time I was the one with my hand up. "Dad, with all due respect, I know I fucked up. And I know I'll probably have to spend the rest of my life on my knees following Chloe around to make up for it. But what I need from you and Mom at this point is support," I told him looking him in the eye. "Because there's no way on earth I'll ever give Chloe a divorce. I've loved that girl my entire life. My earliest life memories are filled with her. No matter what you say, no matter what her father says, no matter how much her mother pleads and no matter how badly her brothers beat the shit out of me, I am not giving Chloe up for anyone. Hell, it doesn't matter what *Chloe* says…I'll never walk away from her, Dad."

He sat there regarding me and the silence was stifling. I meant every word. I didn't need anyone's permission to keep Chloe, but I would love to have their support. After a few tense seconds, my dad let out a deep breath and asked, "Why d'you wait until now to claim her?"

"Because I wanted to have my shit together so I could take care of her," I explained. He was about to speak, so I held up my hand again. "I realize now how stupid my plan was, Dad. I should have married her when we were five and been done with it, but I didn't. And since I can't go back and change the past, all I can do is fix today and hand her my tomorrow."

He sighed. "You know you're going to have to go talk to Anthony and Natalie, right?"

I nodded. "I know, Dad. And I'm more than happy to do it. But back to what I said earlier, it doesn't matter what any of you say, Chloe's mine and I'm not letting her go."

"You know that we all just want you guys to be happy, right?" he asked. "All of you kids. We just want you guys to *all* be happy."

"That won't happen for me, Dad, unless Chloe is with me," I reiterated.

"Go talk with Anthony and Natalie and then come back here for dinner," he instructed. "We'll talk some more then, okay?"

It wasn't his blessing, but it wasn't an uppercut to my kidney, so I'd take it. "Okay, Dad."

He walked me out and gave me a hug as he told me good luck because I was going to need it.

I got to the Slater's a short 20 minutes later and, I'm not going to lie, my palms were sweating, and it felt like my heart was going to pop out of my chest. I had to admit to these people how deeply I hurt their only daughter and the shame was crippling.

I knocked on the door and prayed that they were both here. This shit was painful, and I didn't want to have to confess my sins more times than I had to.

Mrs. Slater opened the door and the look on her face was enough to send me straight back to my car with my tail between my legs. But I didn't run. I stood on her doorstep and prayed that she'd let me in. "Hi, Mrs. Slater. May I come in?"

She sighed, but opened the door to let me in. "Hi, Callum," she replied, her voice sounding heavy. "Why don't you have a seat while I go get Anthony."

I sat down and ran my sweating palms up and down my thighs. I was pretty certain I was going to die, but it wasn't my impending death that bothered me. It was dying before I had a chance to apologize to Chloe and tell her how much I loved her.

I stood up when I heard Mr. and Mrs. Slater entering the room. I waited patiently while Mr. Slater stepped towards me and shook my hand. His face was stoic, and I think he shook my hand out of habit more than anything else.

"Have a seat, Callum," he instructed as he took a seat next to his wife on the couch. I sat on one of the armchairs positioned near the couch. "What can we do for you?"

I winced. I couldn't help it. "Uhm…Chloe told me she spoke with you guys and…well, I was hoping you guys would give me a chance to apologize."

"And what all do you feel you need to apologize for, son?" he asked. He called me 'son'.

*That's a good thing, right?*

And then something nauseating occurred to me. "Uhm, I'm not sure what all Chloe told you gu-"

That's when Mrs. Slater chimed in. "Well, she just told us how you guys got married because she became pregnant as a result of…your guys' indiscretion. Then she went on to explain how you guys weren't living together and your marriage was one of name only."

"She also mentioned how you blamed her for the situation you found yourself in and how she hated you, now, for it," Mr. Slater added, but all I could focus on were his last words. She hated me.

*Chloe hated me.*

I thought I couldn't feel any more desolate than I had when I found out she had lost the baby, but hearing her father tell me that she hated me cut deeper than anything I've ever felt.

I looked her father in the eye and said, "Well, I'm here to tell you everything, sir. And if you ask me to leave and never return, I'll understand." My eyes darted back and forth between Chloe's parents as I added. "But know that nothing you guys say to me, do to me or feel about me will change what Chloe means to me." I cleared my throat. "I'm never going to leave her, and I'll never let her divorce me no matter if I'm on my side alone." They both nodded, and that left me with nothing else to say except to get on with the truth and confess everything.

Neither of them said anything once I was done telling them everything...and I do mean *everything*. I didn't hide how horribly I treated Chloe. The only thing I left out was all the sexual details.

The Slaters exchanged a glance and I could feel my stomach hollow out. They were probably trying to figure out where to bury my body.

It was an agonizing 15 million seconds later that Mr. Slater finally spoke. "Callum," he sighed, "the only reason I'm not calling my sons over here, right now, so we can bury your body in the backyard is because we truly value your parents' friendship."

I couldn't stop the emotion that shot out like a starburst throughout my body.

*They hated me.*

My second set of parents, the people who I've loved and respected my entire life, hated me.

And they were going to try to keep Chloe from me.

"Mr. Slater, Mrs-"

Mrs. Slater put her hand up to stop me, much like my father had earlier when I spoke with him. Disappointment and hurt was evident all over her face. I felt like my entire life was slipping away. If she told Mr. Slater to kill me, I had no doubt he would. But worse, if she told him to keep Chloe away from me, he'd do everything in his power to make that happen. His daughter's happiness was very important to him, but his wife's happiness was paramount. And Mrs. Slater was a mama bear where her children were concerned. She used to be a mama bear towards me, Timothy and Darlene too, but I'm pretty sure I just threw that all away.

"Callum, honey," *Honey?* Was there hope? "As disappointed as we are with how *both* you and Chloe handled this situation, the second, and most important, reason we're not...running you out of our house is because..." She looked over at her husband and I watched as he gave her a tight nod. She returned her gaze back towards me and said, "Chloe's admitted to us how much she loves you, Callum-"

I should have let her continue, but I couldn't stop myself. "She loves me?" I asked, hopefully. "As in...she's in love with me? Not a brotherly sort of love?" God, I sounded desperate and ridiculous.

"She's been in love with you since she was a girl, Callum," Mr. Slater divulged. "And...well, I think you guys both made some mistakes in handling all this. But you have our blessing to try to make it right."

My heart soared, and I was about to fist pump the air, but then Mrs. Slater's next words stopped me. "But make no mistake, Callum," she said, sternly. "If you can't make it up to her, we expect you to let her walk away to find happiness elsewhere. We will not stand by and allow our daughter to live an unhappy existence."

"I understand," I replied. "I do, Mrs. Slater, but…I don't accept those terms." She darted another glance at her husband, but I continued. "Like I stated earlier, Chloe's mine. I'll never, ever let her go. But I can promise to spend every day of the rest of my life making sure she never regrets giving me a second chance." I looked over at Mr. Slater. "I love your daughter, sir. So much so, that breathing won't be possible if she's not in my life."

He reached down to shake my hand, and as soon as I had my hand in his, he drew me up and gave me a hug. I was shocked, emotional and humbled when he said, "That's all we needed to know, son."

I replied with the only thing I knew for sure. "I love her, sir. I love Chloe with everything I am."

## CHAPTER 13

*Chloe*

They finally cleared me to go home, and I was sitting in a wheelchair next to the nurses' station as Callum sorted out some insurance and contact information.

At first, Mya was going to pick me up and take me home, but Callum had called me this morning informing me he was picking me up, and if I didn't want a scene worthy of a YouTube clip, I had better leave with him peacefully. And after yesterday's display of destruction, I heeded his warning.

What surprised the hell out of me was that all morning Callum had been patient and attentive. He had treated me ridiculously delicate when he had helped me out of the bed and into the wheelchair. Every move he made gave the impression that I was more fragile than expensive China. It was sweet, but confusing.

"You ready?" he asked looking down at me.

I just nodded. It felt like there was so much to say, but I couldn't find the right words to even know where to begin. I was still heartbroken over the loss of our baby and, sad to say, I just didn't trust Callum at this point.

It didn't matter how nice he was being this morning. He's been so horrible to me ever since the day I told him I was pregnant, his actions now seemed suspect. Maybe it was guilt.

Maybe he was actually feeling bad because he never wanted this child and he's feeling guilty that, in the light of my obvious sorrow, he's feeling relieved that I miscarried.

I didn't speak as Callum wheeled me out of the hospital and onto the front entrance curb where his car was parked. The second he moved to go open the passenger side door to his car, I grabbed my purse and hospital bag and stood up. I was standing right behind him before he could even turn around, and I could tell by the look on his face, he wasn't happy about me making my own way without his help.

*Well, fuck him.*

He didn't want to be there for me while I was pregnant; I didn't particularly want him to be there for me now that I wasn't. And the more I thought about it, the more I realized I didn't want him to be around me at all. I wasn't sure if I'd ever be able to look at him and not hate how he got his wish.

Callum reached out to support me as I lowered myself into the front seat, but I snatched my arm back, making it clear that I didn't require his assistance. Maybe I was being petty or spiteful, but the more concern he showed, the more pissed off I got.

*How dare he care now.*

How dare he pretend to give a shit now that he was free of a baby I would have given my life for!

I heard him sigh, but he didn't say anything. He just waited for me to buckle myself in before shutting the door and walking around to get into the driver's seat. Callum started the car, pulled out of the loading area and the drive to my apartment was made in complete silence.

Truth be told, it wouldn't have matter who drove me home. I didn't feel like talking to anyone. I just wanted to mourn my loss and try to make sense of what plan God had in place that entailed me to have to go through something like this. I wanted nothing more than to go home, shower, fall into bed and cry myself to sleep. As I stared out the window, I realized a small part of me was happy we hadn't told anyone about the baby. Because we were keeping it a secret, we hadn't bought anything remotely baby related, and I gave a silent thanks for that because I didn't know how I would have handled having to donate any items that I would have had for the baby otherwise.

Callum pulled into the guest spot next to my car, and you better believe, I was out of the car before he had a chance to come around and open my door. I gathered my purse and bag to my chest the best I could with my broken arm and when Callum reached for them, I quickly said, "I got it."

His sigh could have knocked me over. "So, that's how it's going to be then?"

I finally looked up at him. God, how I wanted to punch his beautiful face in. "Not everything is about you, Callum," I retorted. "I'm going to have to manage at work and home with just one arm. That's all I'm doing, right now. Trying to manage."

He didn't say anything more. He just stepped aside to let me pass in front of him. When we reached the lobby of my apartment complex, I noticed he kept following me. I wanted to tell him he didn't need to walk me to my door, but quite frankly, the closer I got to my apartment, the more exhausted I felt. Navigating the stairs had been a struggle.

When we reached the front door to my apartment, I realized just how much of a struggle this was going to be. When you're right-handed, you never realized just how much you use your left hand until you can't use it anymore.

Before I could use my mental super powers to open the door, Callum let out a curse, grabbed my purse from me and fiddled around until he found the keys to my apartment. He unlocked the door and placing his hand on the small of my back, ushered me in. At least he hadn't used his key. I probably would have lost my shit if he had.

"Thank you," I mumbled because I wasn't a complete asshole.

Callum stood in the middle of my apartment and quietly replied, "You're welcome."

I turned away from him and headed towards my bedroom before I made a bigger fool of myself and started crying all over the man.

The only problem?

When I reached my bedroom, it wasn't my bedroom.

I mean, the furniture was all the same. The bedding was still the same. The painted walls were exactly the same shade as before. The bathroom was off to the left like it'd always been. I mean, it *looked* like my room. That is, of course, until you looked over to the opened closet and you saw that one side was completely taken over by suits being held up by hangers and men's shoes on the floor lining the same side.

I rushed over to the nightstand on the side of the bed that I didn't sleep in and pulled the drawers open. *This motherfucker.*

I stomped over to the bathroom, and shit sure enough, there, next to my toothbrush was one that didn't belong. In a slightly manic manner, I started opening every cupboard and pulled out every drawer, and every single time I did, I was greeted by the same sight.

*Callum's shit was everywhere.*

I swung open the shower door and his masculine body wash and what-have-yous were lined along the wall right next to my shampoo, condition and body wash.

All I had wanted to do was come home, take a hot, relaxing bath, cry myself to sleep and find a way to face tomorrow. But now I had to go kick this motherfucker's ass. With a broken arm no less.

I stormed back down the hallway and into the living room only to find this asshole in my kitchen making himself something to eat. I was pissed. I was pissed for a lot of reasons, but he had just given me an outlet for all my twisted, confused emotions. "What the fuck, Callum?"

He turned around, and grabbing the counter behind him, regarded me across the kitchen table. "What now, Chloe?" I noticed his fingers were knuckle-white and gripping the counter's lip.

My eyebrows shot up. "What now?" I damn near screeched. "You know what," I shot back. "What is all your stuff doing here?"

He folded his arms over his chest and my traitorous body noticed how the sinew of his forearms rippled and I wanted to perform an immediate lobotomy on myself. Christ, why did he have to be so damn good in bed?

Today he was wearing a formfitting, blue Henley shirt with dark blue jeans and tan Timberlands. His hair looked like it always did, like some lucky female's been running her hands through those dark, chocolate waves. And that goddamn scar across his cheek was making me want to hold him down and lick his face.

"I moved in," he said, casually, like it was no big deal before turning around to finish making his lunch. "Are you hungry? Oh, I also called the owner of the building and informed him that if that elevator wasn't fixed by the end of the week, you'll be owning it."

I didn't know which shocking statement to address first. "You called the building owner and threatened him?" I went with what was safest.

Callum didn't turn around, but I could tell by the tone of his voice that he was clenching his jaw. "That sonofabitch's neglect cost me my child, Chloe," he spat. "He's lucky that's all I did instead of finding him and beating the ever lovin' fuck out of him!"

My breath hitched. It's the first time he's voiced anything about the loss of our baby. "Call-"

He whirled around and, before I knew it, he was crowding me, peering down at me. "You're not the only one who's mourning, Chloe," he seethed. "That motherfucker is lucky he's still breathing! And as for your original question, I moved in yesterday, and before you say anything, know that I am not in the fucking mood for your shit right now. I'm staying here and I'm going to take care of you no matter how much you want the opposite."

Callum and I always had keys to each other's places, I just never thought he'd abuse the privilege. "Just like that?" I snipped. "I don't have any say?"

He straightened to his full height and looked down at me. "No matter what's transpired in the past couple of days, I'm still your husband, Chloe," he stated, unnecessarily.

I threw my head back and huffed out a laugh I hoped was filled with as much contempt as I felt. "My *husband?* Are you serious?" If Callum was an example of a husband, well, then, God help wives everywhere. "You're not anyone's husband, Callum, least of all, *mine*," I accused. I got up in his face and spewed all the hurt and anguish that's been coursing through my body this past week. "You know what you are? You're nothing but a fucking asshole who can't take responsibility for how and where he sticks his dick. You might have balls the size of Texas in a courtroom, but here, where it matters, you're nothing but a coward, Callum." I could feel tears start coursing down my face, but I didn't care. Fuck. This. Guy. "But do you want to know what really sucks?" I didn't wait for him to answer, nor did I really expect him to. "I wasted 26 years on a friendship that wasn't real," I told him.

His jaw was ticking, and his face took on an unhealthy shade of pink. "What the fuck is that supposed to mean?" he barked.

"It means I realized, now, that we were never friends. We were never anything," I explained through sobs I didn't care to be embarrassed over. "The fact that you thought I was capable of doing all the things you accused me of is proof you never knew me *at all*. And the fact that you did is proof that I never knew you at all either."

"That's bullshit," he snapped as he grabbed me by my arms. "We-"

"No," I interrupted. "What's bullshit is that you would actually think I'd stay married to you now that you little wish has come true!"

Callum let me go and his steps faltered as he moved away from me. His face paled, and he looked as if he'd just been slapped. "My *wish?*"

"Save it, Callum," I spewed. "You never wanted the baby and you sure as hell never wanted to marry me, so don't try to pretend otherwise." And then I said the one thing I knew in my heart to be true. "Don't let my mourning get in the way of your celebrated relief at dodging a bullet. *Two* bullets."

His eyes widened, and he looked like he was going to be sick. "Chloe," he whispered. "Chloe, you can't really believe that…I…"

"I believe you're probably thanking God right now for Mrs. Burks," I insisted.

Callum snapped. "That's bullshit! You know me better-"

"I don't know you *at all!*" I snapped back. "You know what? Just get the hell out of my house, Callum. Leave now and I'll ship your shit to you," I offered right before I said words I never imagined would leave my lips. "And after today, I never want to see your face ever again. Our divorce can be handled though lawyers as far as I'm concerned."

I turned my back on him and headed back towards my bedroom. Any more time in his presence, and I was liable to take back everything I said and beg him to hold me.

I was halfway down the hallway when his bellows reached my ears. "Fuck that, Cee! You'll never be fucking rid of me!" I actually winced because he sounded serious. "I'll never give you a fucking divorce. *Never!*"

I slammed my bedroom door shut on his 'never' and I tried to focus on getting my shit under control instead of the raving lunatic hollering in my living room. Christ, I wouldn't be surprised if the cops showed up at my door with all our noise.

The opened bathroom door caught my attention, and it made me remember that I had wanted to take a hot bath, and so, I latched onto that idea, hoping it would sooth all the hate swirling around in the pit of my stomach.

I toed off my shoes and used my right hand to remove my socks. Once those were off, I headed towards the bathroom and did my best to wiggle out of my pants. By the time I was kicking them away, I had broken out in a light sweat and my breathing was labored. I couldn't stop the tears when I took off the sling and wondered how I was going to pull off my t-shirt. Mya had brought me a change of clothes at the hospital to make me more comfortable, but right now, I wasn't comfortable at all.

Suddenly, all my emotions felt like they were battering me from every direction. I dropped to the floor and just started crying until it was painful to even catch my breath.

I cried for everything I lost. My baby, my friend, my hopes at a lifetime marriage like my parents. The joy at ever getting pregnant again. I mean, how can I ever get pregnant again without reliving the pain of losing my very first child ever?

I cried at not being able to get a simple t-shirt off.

And the one person who can make it all go away sat in my living room mad at me because I didn't want anything to do with him.

# CHAPTER 14

*Callum*

*Karma's a motherfucker.*

That's all I could think when I replayed her words back in my head. Chloe had accused me of things I never thought she'd think I was capable of…much like I had done to her.

And it stung.

It stung like a sonofabitch.

If this was any kind of window into how I had been making her feel these past few months, no wonder she hated me.

I was hurting at our loss also, but she didn't believe that. And to be fair, I never gave her a reason to believe it.

Regret was like a demonic hand wrapping around my throat threatening to ruin the rest of my life.

And just when I hadn't thought I could feel any worse, Chloe had to go denounce our entire life together.

She said we've never been friends, and that gutted me like nothing else. Losing our child was close, but to hear Chloe yell away most of my childhood memories had been brutal.

She *was* my childhood, and she didn't even know it because I was a dumbass.

It wasn't until I sat down, closed my eyes and threw my head back on the couch that I could make out her cries. They were faint, but I could hear them all the same.

I stood up to go to her because I wasn't going to be that guy. I wasn't going to be the dick who sat in the other room as she cried out her misery. Whether she wanted me to or not, I wasn't going to leave her alone to suffer whatever she was going through alone.

A lot of people advise giving your woman space-and make no mistake, Chloe *was* my woman-but I always thought that was just a cop out to avoid having to deal with a woman's complex emotions. Throughout the years whenever a friend would tell me he was giving his girl time to cool off, I always wondered how the girl felt knowing her man was off nursing a beer somewhere while she was left alone to cry and sort out her feelings on her own.

It always seemed sucky to me. Even when I followed Andrew's advice about giving Chloe some space after our wedding night, I knew deep down it hadn't been the best idea. Chloe was the type that needed space, but not while she was hating me.

Besides, I deserved whatever Chloe wanted to dish out at me. Even though she was wrong about everything, she was entitled to her rage and regret. I had been a dick.

I made my way to her bedroom and because the bathroom door was open, I immediately saw her sitting on the floor, her shirt tangled all around her, crying.

*I deserved to get my ass kicked by her brothers.*

I knelt down in front of her and reached to remove her shirt. She looked up at me and the look in her bright blues would have been enough to send me to my knees if I hadn't already been on them. "Chloe…"

"I *hate* you, Callum," she whispered brokenly, and I believed her.

"I know, Cee," I whispered back, because I did know.

And then she continued to slice me open when she sobbed, "Make it go away, Callum. Make it *all* go away. *Please…*"

I removed her shirt and gathered her in my arms until she was curled up in my lap, both of us on the floor. She was in nothing but her panties, and I felt like a heel noticing. Chloe was sitting broken in my arms and my dick was registering how perfect her body felt pressed up against mine.

"I'm sorry, Cee," I whispered in her hair. I knew she didn't believe me, or even cared to hear what I had to say, but it was the truth. I was so *goddamn sorry*.

She didn't comment. She just kept crying into my neck and I just kept holding her. I felt like such a fucking hypocrite knowing that had it been any other man who made her cry like this, I would have kicked his ass. But it was me. I'm the one who did this to her.

*And it was fucking killing me.*

"Tell me what to do, Chloe," I implored. "I'll do anything to make it better for you."

She pulled back from me and looked up into my face. She was a beautiful mess. "I want a bath," she said surprising me. And then not surprising me, she continued, "I want a bath and then a divorce."

I ran my hand up her neck to cradle her face. I searched those blue pools of hers and I knew I was just going to make things worse, but I couldn't stop myself. There's no way I would let her believe that was an option, even if it was just to help make her feel better. "A bath I can do, Cee," I replied. "But I meant it when I said I'll never give you a divorce." She closed her eyes as if the last of her hope was fading away. "You're mine, Chloe. You've always been mine and you'll always be mine. Even if you hate me for the rest of our days, I'll still never let you go."

She opened her eyes, and she looked genuinely confused. *"Why?"*

I let out a sigh. She deserved to know the truth, but not like this. Not with her half naked on the floor. "Why don't we get you into the shower and we can talk later?" I studied her precious, sorrowful face. "I promise we'll talk once you're-"

Tears started to gather, and she mumbled, "I can't shower with my arm all…"

I didn't know how I was going to do it, but I was. No matter what it took. No matter how much everything male in me would protest. I was going to bathe her and take care of her *without* fucking her up against the shower wall. There was no way she was emotionally or physically capable of resisting me-which I knew she'd *want* to-and that was a little too close to rape for my conscience.

"Let's stand up and give me a second." She let me help her stand and once she was steady on her feet, I headed for the kitchen to get a trash bag. Luckily, I knew where everything was. I knew Chloe's apartment like I knew my own home.

I grabbed one of the small trashcan liners and when I made it back to the bathroom, she silently let me wrap the bag around her cast and tie it as tight as I could without cutting off the circulation to her arm. "Thank you," she mumbled, and I knew it cost her to say it. I knew it was killing her to accept any help from me, whatsoever, right now. But I was grateful. She'd never know just how grateful I was for her compliance right now.

I walked over to the shower and turned on the water, adjusting the temperature to the exact combination of cold and hot that she liked. I knew she preferred a bath, but we didn't fit in the tub together and I wasn't leaving her alone. I tested the water, and with all the stress she was feeling, she probably wanted it a little hotter, but what she didn't know was that I was going to be the one to relieve her stress, not a goddamn hot shower.

After getting the water just right, I started removing my clothes. Chloe's eyes widened the second she realized what I was doing, but she didn't object, and I wasn't entirely sure if that was a good thing or not. Either she wasn't objecting because she was too exhausted to fight, or she wasn't objecting because she really was done with me and wasn't afraid of any sexual attraction lingering about.

*God, I hope it's the former.*

Once I was completely naked, I walked towards her, and reaching for her panties, I went to pull them down. They were the only thing still on her. But the second my hands touched the elastic band of her underwear, her hands clamped down on mine, stopping me.

I looked up at her and the look on her face nearly did me in. "What's wrong, baby?"

Silent sobs started to wrack her body, and in a voice that sliced right through me, she said, "I…I'm bl…bleeding. It's…I'm a m…m…mess."

I had to turn away. I couldn't look at her. I couldn't face what I'd done to her. Because she could call it a tragic accident all she wanted, but I knew differently. If I hadn't been such a fucking cunt, she would have been living with me from the second she told me she was pregnant, and she would never have been in this goddamn building where the elevator doesn't work.

And it fucking killed me that, after all the countless times I've run to the store to pick up tampons for her, she thought I gave a fuck that she was bleeding. She was embarrassed, and after all we've been through together, that's the last thing Chloe should ever feel around me.

I forced myself to look back up at her because I deserved to feel the stabbing in my chest. I couldn't hide the fury in my voice though. The fury at myself. "I don't give a fuck if you're bleeding or not, Cee," I growled. She turned her head, her face flushed, clearly embarrassed. "And you better get used to it because once we're back on track…back where we're supposed to be, your goddamn period isn't going to stop me from fucking you when I need to be inside you."

Chloe gasped, and her head snapped back down as she stared at me with big, wide doe eyes. "Callum, you-"

I ignored her and turned my attention to her panties. "Now, work with me," I said, interrupting whatever she was about to object to.

To my utter surprised, Chloe placed her right hand on my shoulder and lifted her feet accordingly, so I could remove her panties. The fucked-up thing about it though? When she said it, the words all made sense in my head, but I wasn't prepared to see the pad filled with blood in the lining of her underwear.

I blinked away the moisture the sight brought to my eyes, though. I needed to be here for Chloe, not for anything I deserved to feel.

I stood up and walked her over to the shower. Once she was inside standing underneath the spray, I removed the pad from her panties, rolled it up, threw it away and dropped her panties on top of the pile of her discarded clothes.

When I looked up over at Chloe, I saw a faint, pink hue swirling around the drain and I wondered just how much more I could take.

I stepped into the shower with her, and placing my hands on her shoulders, I turned her around until she was facing the showerhead with her back towards me. I grabbed her bottle of shampoo, and after squeezing a handful into my palm, I placed it back in its spot and got to washing Chloe's hair.

Everything in me wanted to do a victory punch in the air when she dropped her head back, let out a little moan, and didn't fight me on this.

We didn't speak as she let me wash her hair and massage her scalp and, at one point, she even had to slap a hand against the tiled wall to stay upright. I hoped that meant I was doing a good job.

Once I was done, I turned her around, rinsed out the shampoo and repeated the same steps to condition her hair. Only this time, I let the conditioner sit in her hair as I grabbed that scrunchie thing, poured some of her body wash on it, and proceeded to wash every inch of her skin. It was after that, that I positioned her underneath the showerhead again and rinsed her hair clean of the conditioner. I laughed to myself how I knew to do that.

Over the years, I've learned all about Chloe's little habits and idiosyncrasies. And somewhere during our friendship, she must have mentioned the tricks to conditioning a woman's hair, because I knew she needed it to sit a few minutes to help with the tangles.

*Jesus, the crazy shit I knew because of this woman.*

Now, this is where it got tricky. I saved the inside of Chloe's thighs for last because, while I knew about her shampoo and conditioner habits, I wasn't sure what to do about her bleeding. It made sense in my head to save that for last because had I washed down there first, she could still bleed, needing me to wash her again, right?"

My heart was thumping a painful tattoo inside my chest, scared as fuck I was going to undo any progress I might have made with her while she let me wash her. I didn't let it stop me, though.

I squeezed a shitload of my body wash in my hand, and it didn't escape my notice at just how sick in the head I was that I was using my body wash instead of hers because I wanted her pussy to smell like me. The way I figured, she could damn well smell like me while she was out of commission. Once she was completely healed and madly in love with me, she could go back to smelling like *us*.

Holding her stare, I lathered the body wash in my hands and reaching down, I, oh, so very softly, ran my fingers back and forth from her dark, wet curls trimmed over her clit, to her clit, through her folds and all the way back to that puckered little hole I've been dying to sink into.

I cleaned around every hidden crevice, making sure my eyes didn't leave her face. I didn't want to miss the second she got uncomfortable or upset. But Chloe quietly let me clean her, and when I was done, I turned her around letting the water run down her body. I used my hand to help the water rid her of any residual traces of soap. Plus, it gave me a few precious seconds to will my dick to go down.

*The motherfucker had no sense of what was appropriate and what wasn't.*

I got out of the shower first and quickly dried off. After wrapping the towel around my waist, I grabbed another towel and helped Chloe out of the shower. I dried her body off, unwrapped the plastic from around her cast and then covered her with the towel.

"Wait right here," I told her right before I headed into the bedroom to grab her a pair of panties. Thank God I knew where she kept everything.

I hurried back into the bathroom, opened the bottom righthand drawer and pulled out one of her pads. I knew enough about Chloe to know that every now and again her periods were so heavy she had to use tampons with a pad as backup. She confessed that bit of personal information when we were 16 years old and I tried to convince her to go to a river party with me. She cried out in frustration-or PMS-why she couldn't risk going swimming. So, we had ended up staying in her room watching movies.

Not caring if I looked like an idiot, I unwrapped two pads and placed them inside her panties how I thought they should go. And avoiding her gaze, I walked up to her and knelt down to pull them up her legs.

The entire time, Chloe hadn't uttered a word, but the silence was deafening. I felt like a complete fool doing this for her, but not because I was embarrassed, but because I knew she didn't want my help.

Well, that was until I stood up and finally found the balls to look at her.

Chloe's eyes were shimmering with tears, but she had the smallest tilt to lips. She looked like she wanted to smile but was still very aware of how much she hated me. But then she surprised the fuck out of me when she pushed her body into mine and stood there letting me wrap my arms around her.

She let me hold her for about 20 seconds before saying, "I still hate you, Callum."

My arms tightened around her body. "I know you do, Cee."

A few quiet seconds later, she said, "Okay. It's time to talk."

# CHAPTER 15

*Chloe*

I was so goddamn exhausted, I wasn't even sure I was up for 'the talk' with Callum.

After our shower, Callum had brushed my wet hair and piled it on top of my head with a purple scrunchie. Once my hair was taken care of, he dressed me in a plain, white t-shirt and pajama shorts and then dressed himself in a pair of lounge pants. It was the middle of the day, but I had no plans to leave the house and so I guess that meant he didn't either. I wasn't sure what he was doing about work, but one day off wasn't going to hurt him any. Callum was Clayton, Nelson & Moreno's new golden boy.

And, now, I was sitting on the couch, watching him make me a cup of tea and waiting for him to say whatever it is he feels he has to say.

I wasn't going to lie to myself and act like I wasn't a million different kinds of confused, because I was. And maybe I wasn't in a good emotional place to be having any kind of serious talks with Callum, but if nothing else, we needed to discuss what we were going to do about our marriage.

I know he said he wouldn't grant me a divorce, but I was chalking that up to him being wrapped up in his emotions just like I was. People say all kinds of crazy stuff when they're losing their shit.

As I watched him move around my kitchen with such ease and familiarity, I couldn't help but replay how he knew where my underwear was kept and how he knew where my tampons and pads were. I was so painfully hurt, but the tightness in my chest as I watched him place two pads inside the lining of my underwear, wasn't from my pain or his betrayal.

It had been from regret.

I was witnessing exactly how Callum would treat his real wife someday and it broke whatever pieces of my heart were left. And then I was hit with the reminder of how we were no longer best friends and I resented him knowing me so well in that moment.

Maybe now really isn't a good time to have a heart to heart. Just because I no longer have the energy to be raging mad, doesn't mean that I'm still not. I had missed calls from both Mya and my parents, and while I called them each back when Callum first went off to make me some tea, maybe I should have taken them up on their offers to go stay with them.

*Maybe I'm just a goddamn coward.*

I didn't have any more time to think on it because apparently my tea was done and Callum was already making his way towards me.

My heart sank at how beautiful he was.

He placed my tea on the coffee table, and I saw that he had water for himself. My throat worked a rough swallow as Callum sat down next to me, and in a habit as old as time itself, he grabbed my legs and threw them over his lap, maneuvering me to rest against the armrest of the couch as he leaned up against the backrest.

I cringed at how good it felt to feel his hands running up and down over my legs. I didn't want to enjoy his touch. I wanted to hate him. I wanted to hate him so goddamn much.

"How are you feeling?" he asked and then seemed to catch himself. "I mean, how are you feeling physically? Did the shower help?"

I just stared at him. I honestly didn't know how to answer the man.

In all actuality, I didn't want to answer him. I wanted to yell at him. I wanted to blame him for everything. I wanted to hurt him. I wanted to unleash all my pain onto him. I wanted him to carry some of the weight of all the emotions threatening to drown me.

"Chloe…" he sighed.

*Fuck it.*

If he wanted to talk…well, then we'll talk.

"No, the shower didn't help, Callum. Every so often I can feel blood leaking from my body reminding me that I'll probably need another shower soon," I said, cruelly. "And all the shower did was remind me that I'm no longer pregnant as I watched the red-tinted water run down the drain beneath me." I could feel myself losing it. "So, no, Callum. The shower *didn't. Fucking. Help!*"

His hands gripped my legs, and the pressure wasn't subtle. "Chloe-"

I didn't let him finish. Staring right into his baby browns, I continued my rant, "But you got what you wanted, right? You said you were mourning, too, but we both know your heart is probably dancing a little jig over not having to be saddled with a kid you never wanted and a wife you would have never picked for yourself."

"That's not fucking true!" Apparently, the gloves were off. "I get it, okay?" Callum ranted. "I get it now. I get how it feels to be accused of…being someone you're not. Of wanting or doing something that's not true." His eyes conveyed pure agony and his face looked pained. "I know you hadn't gotten pregnant on purpose," he said, surprising me. "And I also know it's too late to make that believable. I know you'll always think I'm saying this, now, because you...because we lost the baby." His hands squeezed my legs like I was the only thing holding him together. "And I'm also very aware that you're going to think that everything I'm saying now is because of what we're going through, but I can't help that. I can't control that, no matter how much I might want to."

"Cal-"

He didn't let me talk. "So, I'm going to say what I have to say, and you can believe me or not, but my words, your doubt...none of it will affect whether we stay married or not. Because, Chloe, we are not getting a divorce. Ever."

My heart was thumping in my chest. I'm not going to lie. A small part of me took joy in knowing that the shoe was on the other foot. Now, it was Callum trying to convince me that he wasn't low enough for the things I accused him of feeling. Now, it was him trying to prove his dignity existed.

"I love you, Chloe. I-"

*Ugh*. How typical. I knew he loved me. We'd been best friends our entire lives. "I know you do, Callum. I know-"

He shook his head at me, and took me by surprise when he reached out, grabbed my shoulders and pulled me into his lap. He had his arms wrapped around me while I was curled up and nestle against the chest I longed to lick.

Callum kissed the top of my head before continuing, "No, Cee. I'm not saying I love you like I love your parents or your brothers. I'm not saying I love you like I love the girl who sports the same scar across her face as I do."

My eyes watered. I wasn't completely sure, but I had a scary feeling of where he was going with this. Scary because the hope I was beginning to feel was dangerous. What if I was wrong about the type of love I was dying to hear? "No?"

He tightened his hold on me. "No, Chloe. I love you like I'm in love with the only girl-woman I have ever loved." I started crying. "I've loved you since we were old enough to talk. But I've been in love with you since we were ten years old. I love you and I've always been in love with you. Hell, I'll always be in love with you. You were always going to be my wife. Always."

"Then why, Callum?" I got out between sobs. Why would he be so damn cruel if he was in love with me?

He let out a sad, little huff of a laugh. "Because I'm a fucking idiot, Cee." I didn't comment because...well, what's there to say? He is. "I'm going to tell you something, and even though I don't deserve it, I'm asking you to just listen. Don't react. Don't argue. Don't do anything but just listen and try to hear what I'm telling you. Can you do that for me? *Will* you do that for me?"

While he was right-he didn't deserve any kind of compassion or understanding from me-he was still the boy who played with me when my brothers didn't want their little sister tagging along behind them. He was still the boy who shared the same scar I did and didn't rat me out when my scar was a genuine accident and his was an act of revenge. And-call me a fool-but three months of utter misery didn't undo 26 years of happiness at the hands of this jackass.

So, I agreed to listen.

"Okay," I whispered, my sobs ending.

"My earliest memories I have of life have you in them. You were my best friend for as long as I've known existence. At ten, when I started noticing that girls were different from boys in more ways than one, I knew you were going to be the girl I was going to have a family with. I would look at our parents and I knew that you were that person. When we got older, you were going to be that for me."

Every word he spoke chilled the fire of hate I was feeling towards him and I cursed agreeing to listen to him. I wanted to stay mad at him. "Okay…"

His arm left arm tightened around my back as his right hand started rubbing up and down my outer thigh. "When we turned 13 and puberty was at its inception, I wanted my first everything to be with you, but I was scared. You weren't meant to fool around with. By then, I knew without a doubt, that you were going to be my wife one day and I was not going to do anything in the meantime to jeopardize that."

"Callum-"

"Shh," he teased. "You said you would listen."

I didn't mean to, but I chuckled. This was the Callum I knew and loved. "Okay. You may continue," I teased back.

I could feel him take a deep breath before continuing, "All throughout our teenage years, it was more of the same. I wanted you, but I was going to do it right. I was going to let you live and do some living of my own. We were going to graduate, go off to college, get our shit together and…" He stopped and let out the most pitiful laugh.

"And what?" I was dying to see how this was going to end.

"I figured once I had everything under control and I was settled in my career, I was going to ask you to marry me. You were going to say yes-because…of course. We'd be married within a year or so, you'd be pregnant a year after that until we had at least four kids and then just live happily ever after."

I listened to his words like I promised I was going to, but they didn't make any sense. How could he have all this planned, but I knew nothing about it? He tells me all this as if it was an actual given. So many things could have happened in 26 years that could have derailed his plans. "And what would you have done had I been dating someone when you were ready to finally ask me to marry you? Or if one of my past boyfriends had asked me to marry him and I'd said yes?"

Callum snorted in true arrogance. "I would have changed his mind really quick, Chloe. I don't care who he would have been. You were mine. You were always meant to be mine. All those guys, all those girls…they were always meant to just be temporary."

I was kind of nonplussed at this moment.

After a few quiet seconds, I just had to ask, "Do you realize how arrogant that sounds?"

His hand squeezed the top of my thigh. "Yes," he answered. "But it doesn't make it any less the truth."

I decided not to go up against his mental defect. Instead, I asked the question I really wanted the answer to. "So, why these last couple of months, Callum?"

"I meant what I said earlier. It's because I'm an idiot. I was so *pissed,* Cee. So goddamn pissed off when you told me you were pregnant because...because it ruined my plans. I hated thinking that you would always believe I married you because you were pregnant when, in reality, you're the love of my life, and I've always wanted to marry you. I didn't think you'd believe me if I told you I was marrying you for love and not for the baby."

*Wow.*

That is not the answer I was expecting.

Not. At. All.

"I don't know what to say." I really didn't. I mean...this was some crazy shit. I would have never imagined that the reason Callum had been so hateful was because his plans of the perfect proposal had been ruined. "You know how psychotic that sounds?"

I felt his chest vibrate against my face as he laughed. "Yeah, now that I hear myself, it does sound a bit unstable."

"A bit?"

Callum used his hands to maneuver me into a straddling position over his lap. He cradled my face as he said, "I don't want to insult you by telling you I'm sorry, because there's no apology big enough to make up for everything I've done to you. Everything I've caused."

I knew he was talking about losing the baby. And I wanted to be the bigger person and assure him that it was all just a horrible life trial, but I didn't. I didn't because we were both to blame for the loss of our baby. Had we'd really been doing what was right for this baby, we would have behaved way differently, and I might have never been in the path of that desk.

My only saving grace was that I do believe in The Lord and His plan. Our baby wasn't meant to be-for whatever reason-and I had to hold on to that or I'd lose my damn mind.

It was going to take me a long time to heal from this, but right now, I had to concentrate on my life as it was and where I was going to go from here. "So, what now?"

He leaned forward and kissed the tip of my nose. When he leaned back, he ran his thumbs back and forth over cheeks and said, "Now you let me take care of you and try to find some way to make everything up to you." His eyes looked so sad as he pleaded with me. "I know nothing will make losing the baby better, but I want to try to make us better, Cee."

"Callu-"

He shook his head at me, stopping me from speaking. "Let me do this, Chloe." He placed a soft kiss on my lips. "Please, just let me love you and give me a chance to try to make up for being a complete asshole. *Please.*"

My pride was telling me he didn't deserve a chance to love me. The ache of my loss was telling me he didn't deserve a chance to make it right because…well, he couldn't.

But my mind was telling me that-to be fair-nothing was going to make the ache go away. And my heart…my heart was telling me that the ache was definitely never go away, but maybe Callum would help make it less painful.

I decided to listen to my heart.

## CHAPTER 16

*Callum*

I wasn't sure how much more distance I could take.

After our talk on Thursday, Chloe agreed to not hate me as much as she had the right to. It wasn't exactly a fast track to undying love, but I was smart enough to take what I could get from her right now.

She had slept on and off most of Thursday, but the nurse had said as much when she explained Chloe's aftercare to me. And then Friday was spent with her family and Mya visiting her and making sure she was okay.

The day was painfully and awkwardly…careful, but it hadn't been terribly bad. At least, it hadn't been until Mrs. Burks came knocking on the door. By the time she was done crying and begging for forgiveness, I had put aside all my regret and resentment and wanted to do nothing more than comfort the older woman.

We hadn't uttered a word about Chloe's pregnancy because Mrs. Burks didn't need to know. She was so terribly sorry if she knew Chloe had been pregnant, I don't think the woman would have been able to live with herself.

There was also the glaring double-edge sword of construction noise that we hadn't been able to drown out. All day Friday, construction crews and handymen were coming and going into the building fixing up everything. And I do mean *everything*.

The elevator, of course, but there were men everywhere touching up paint, replacing door hinges, insulating windows, all kinds of odd shit. I guess the owner of the building took me seriously when I told him Chloe would be owning this place by the end of the month if he didn't make shit right.

In all actuality, it seemed kind of pointless now. As soon as Chloe felt better, I had every intention of moving her into my place. The fact of the matter was, I planned on getting her pregnant again very soon, and my place was bigger. Yeah, it lacked warmth, but once Chloe moved all her shit in, it would start feeling like a home. *Our* home.

Of course, that meant Mya and I would have to come to some sort of mutual cease fire for Chloe's sake. I had no plans on giving Chloe up and I knew Mya wasn't going to either, not that I would want or expect that. Chloe needed a best friend; I wasn't going to begrudge her that. Besides, I no longer wanted to be her best friend. I wanted to be more important than her best friend. Best friends could be replaced-evident by Mya's and Andrew's existences-but a husband is supposed to be an only and onetime deal.

I had fucked this up pretty epically from the get-go, but I was determined to make myself irreplaceable in Chloe's life. I was going to make it so that she wouldn't know how to live without me by her side. I was going to make her addicted to my presence.

At least, I was hoping to.

The biggest struggle I had was my conscience. If Chloe wanted to really walk away from me, I wouldn't blame her. I didn't deserve her. She'd have every right to turn away from me and find happiness with someone else. Someone who's never hurt her or betrayed her at the level that I had. Problem with that was, it didn't matter how much my mind knew letting her walk was the right thing to do, my heart, body and soul were like *'fuck that shit!'* And since they outnumbered my mind and its conscience, Chloe wasn't going anywhere in life without me.

So, my only option was to do what I should have done a long time ago. I'm going to date my wife and hope she's receptive to my attempts to start the courting phase of our relationship over again.

I heard water start flowing through the pipes and I recognized the sound of her starting a bath. The sound resonated differently inside the walls than when the shower was on.

I threw the blanket off the lower half of my body and sat up on the couch. Even though all my stuff was in her bedroom and bathroom, she hadn't invited me to sleep in her bed and I hadn't asked. She can take this as slow as she needs, and I'll stick to her pace.

The worst part was that I've slept with Chloe countless times in her bed with her. We've slept together in my bed together, at our parents' houses together, camping...a million different places. She's slept in my arms more than any other person on earth. And that included all the times I crawled into my parents' bed when I was little.

And now I slept on her couch-which was way too short for my body-waiting for Chloe to come around and trust me again. Actually, *praying* for Chloe to come around and trust me again. *Motherfucker, did I pray.*

I stood up, stretched, yawned and adjusted my junk before folding the blanket and stacking it neatly on top of my pillow. I left them on the edge of the couch knowing I'll be using them again tonight. I contemplated buying a rollaway bed and cramming it into her spare bedroom. She used it as an office, but there was room for a small rollaway. The couch just wasn't large enough and I couldn't keep waking up with all these aches and pains.

Suddenly, a hot shower sounded perfect. Since Chloe was taking a bath, me running a shower shouldn't bother her. She was done running the hot water necessary for her bath. So, I walked right through the bedroom and opened the bathroom door like she wasn't on the other side.

My eyes found her immediately as I walked in and her eyes rounded at the sight of me. Her beautiful body was hidden underneath a layer of lavender-scented bubbles, and while bubble bath had never wronged me in the past, I hated its very existence in this moment as it covered Chloe's body.

"What the hell, Callum?" she screeched. "What are you doing in here?"

I shrugged a shoulder and started removing my t-shirt and lounge pants as if this was the norm. "I'm going to take a hot shower," I answered. "That couch is too small for me and it's killing my shoulders and my back." She just blinked at me. "I figured since you were in the bath, I could run a shower without hogging all the hot water." Her face turned pink as soon as I kicked my pants off my left ankle, and I was standing before her completely naked. I willed my dick to stay soft, but it was a struggle.

"Bu…but, uhm…" She started gnawing at the left side of her bottom lip, but I just waited patiently for her to finish speaking. Her eyes were cast downwards when she said, "I'm still bleeding. I…uh, planned on just using the bath to relax. I was going to take a proper shower afterwards."

I had to swallow. I knew she was still healing, and sex was the last thing on her mind, but I couldn't stop the image of Chloe dripping wet in the shower with me. I appreciated every chance I got when it came to being able to see her naked body.

I lost the struggle with my dick, and within seconds, it was standing at full attention. Thankfully, Chloe's eyes were still staring at the bubbles in her bath, though. I turned and walked into the shower. "Then you can join me when you're done," I said, trying to sound as casual as possible. "If not, I promise to save some hot water for you."

I got in the shower, turned on the water and adjusted it to my liking. I stood under the spray and let the hot water pelt my neck, shoulders and back. Half of me prayed Chloe would stay in the bathtub until I was finished with my shower, while the other half, prayed she'd join me.

It was a torturous game my mind played with, constantly thinking of all the different ways I wanted Chloe, and then remembering all the reasons I couldn't have her.

Just yet, that is.

I was just getting ready to reach for my shampoo bottle when I heard the telltale noised of the bathtub drain being opened and the water starting to swirl down the pipes. I let out a deep breath and thanked God for that small miracle. Either, Chloe was getting out of the tub and saving her bath for another time, leaving me to shower in peace, or she was joining me.

I prayed she was joining me.

That prayer came true a few seconds later when I turned to watch her open the shower door and walk in, closing it behind her.

Chloe was naked, dripping wet with bubbles still randomly clinging to her body. Her brown tresses were still knotted in a bun on top of her head, and I wanted so badly to be the man who had permission to reach over and let her hair down.

"I didn't want to take any chances with the hot water," she whispered like it was wrong for her to be in here with me.

I hated that.

I wanted her to know she belonged anywhere I was.

So, I reached for her hair tie, pulled it out of her hair as gently as I could, and started running my fingers through her scalp as I watched her hair fall down her back. It was a beautiful thing to be able to do, but my mind automatically went to replay the images of all the times I had those silky strands wrapped around my fist as I fucked everything I had into her body.

My dick was hating me right now.

"You know," I reached for her shoulders and I switched our places so she was now standing under the water, "you don't have to give me a reason for why you're in here." I secured her hair tie around my wrist and I was pretty sure I was going to leave it there.

Forever.

Chloe closed her eyes and tilted her head back underneath the showerhead. I watched as the water cascaded down her body and removed all the bubble bath suds that had been clinging to her body.

My dick was *really, really* hating me.

"I'm not sure if I still hate you or not," she replied, snapping me out of my perusal of her naked body.

I looked at her and her eyes were now opened, looking at me. I reached for her shampoo and went to work on squeezing some into my hands. I twirled my finger around, giving her the universal signal to turn around and, as soon as she did, I started washing her hair. I needed time to think about how I wanted to respond to her little announcement.

She deserved to be able to hang onto her anger and still hate me, but I didn't want to feed it and help it grow. "As long as you feel something towards me, I'll take it, Cee," I responded, honestly. "But just know, it doesn't matter if you hate me or not, I'm not going anywhere."

"You're okay with me hating you for the rest of our lives?" she asked as she continued to let me wash her hair.

"I'm hoping, one day, you'll realize how exhausting it is to hate every day-day in and day out, and you'll forgive me." I turned her around and stuck her head back underneath the showerhead to rinse the shampoo out.

She didn't say anything for a while and I didn't know if that was a good thing or a bad thing. When she finally spoke, I thought my knees were going to give out.

Chloe's hair was free of shampoo, but she made no effort to move onto the next step of her routine shower. Instead, she planted her hands on my chest and ran them upward until she was playing with my collarbone.

My hands automatically went to her hips.

"I love you, Cee." Chloe closed her eyes really quickly and shook her head. "No. No, that's not right." She looked back up at me and her gorgeous green eyes were filled with determination, strength and, yes, a little bit of hate still. "I love you, Callum. I've always loved you as Cee, my best friend. But, somewhere along the way, I fell in love with you as Callum. As the man who I really wanted to marry and grow old with."

"Chl-"

"Let me finish," she commanded. And, so, I let her. "I'm in so much pain right now, I can't say I'm capable of thinking straight or making any good decisions. I harbor so much regret, anger, pain and sadness that I can't tell where one emotion begins and the other one ends." She was gutting me wide open. "Your words are going to forever haunt me, you know. Your accusations, your opinion of me, after all the years we've known each other…they're going to haunt me. They're going to make me doubt everything I ever thought was real between us."

"I already explained why I was being so hateful, Chloe," I replied, wanting to shut her the fuck up because her words were motherfucking killing me. "I knew…I *know* you're not that type of pers-"

"It doesn't matter that you've explained that now, Callum," she said, interrupting me. "For months I believed you thought that of me and that changed everything I ever felt about you." She looked up at me and her face looked so agonized. "Can you understand that? Do you get how I spent every minute of every day for the past couple of months slowing changing how I felt about you? How I saw you?"

I could feel the cold settling in the marrow of my bones. I was losing her.

Hell, I think I've already *lost* her. There was no losing about it.

I was about to drop to my knees and just start fucking begging when her next words stopped me cold. "But I'm still attracted to you, Callum. I still think about that first night together and our wedding night." Her hands started running up and down my chest. "Sex and love are two very different things; they don't necessarily have to go hand in hand. So, here's my proposal. I'm willing to stay married to you for the time being and, once the doctor gives me the okay, I'm willing to continue having sex with you."

This wasn't good. I knew it. I felt it. "But…"

"I don't trust you," she blatantly stated. "And I have every intention of trusting the man I plan on spending the rest of my life with, so that man isn't going to be you."

I let go of her hips and took a couple of steps back, the shower all but forgotten. "What the fuck does that mean?"

"I'll stayed married to you and continue to sleep with you until I've exhausted all my hate, regret, pain and mourning. I want to use you to heal, and once I'm done healing, I want a divorce and I want to move on with someone who will know the real me and love me with no past, no pain, no regret, no sorrow, no remorse…no nothing. I want to find someone I can trust with my happiness."

"You said…you said you would give me a chance to make it up to you," I said, reminding her of our conversation the day she came home from the hospital.

"I changed my mind," she said simply, as if she wasn't carving out my soul.

"Okay," I replied. I couldn't think of anything else to say. It felt like I couldn't breathe, and I'd die of suffocation if I tried to utter more than just that one word.

This was all too much. I gave her a slight nod and, my shower forgotten, I stepped out of the shower, grabbed a towel and headed towards the bedroom.

Ten minutes later, I had my keys in hand and was walking out the front door.

# CHAPTER 17

*Chloe*

When I heard the front door shut quietly behind Callum's exit, I knew something had seriously changed between us.

I was woman enough to acknowledge what I did, and that's why Mya was now sitting on the couch next to me. I needed some serious advice.

"Why would you tell him that after giving him the impression you were willing to work things out…get past all his bullshit?" Mya asked, genuinely confused.

I couldn't ask her for advice if I wasn't completely honest with her. "I got scared," I confessed.

Mya cocked her head and drew her brows in. "Of what, Chloe?"

"Of making the wrong decision, Mya."

"About what?" She truly looked confused. She was looking at me like I had an extra ear growing out of my forehead and she didn't have the faintest idea what to do about it.

"About Callum," I moaned. "I want to forgive him and go on to live happily ever after, but he doesn't deserve to be forgiven, Mya. He treated me horribly and what if he does it again?"

Her eyes bugged out. "Again?" she asked. "What? You plan on having another drunken one-night stand with him where you get pregnant and are forced to marry him again?" Mya let out an incredulous laugh. "Because, I gotta tell you, Chloe, if you are, then let me get a camera crew together and start our own reality show because that shit would be nuts."

I stink-eyed her as I tossed one of the throw pillows at her. "Quit being a jerk, Mya," I laughed. "I'm trying to pour my heart out to you, you whore."

Mya smiled, but it was filled with the tenderness she was always demonstrating. "Chloe, I know you're still pissed at Callum and a part of you wants him to hurt the same way he hurt you, bu-"

"It's not that," I said, interrupting her. "It's…" *God, this sucked.* "Forgiving him without making him pay for everything he did to me makes me feel weak."

Mya let out a deep breath. "Chloe, forgiveness doesn't make you weak. It actually reinforces how strong you are." She reached out and took my hands in hers. "Do you realize how brave a person has to be to experience heartbreak and still put themselves out there to possibly experience it again?" She let go of my hands and leaned back against the armrest. "That's real strength, Chloe."

"Then why does it make me feel stupid?" Every time I thought about falling into Callum's arm, I felt like the biggest fool.

"Okay, let's be practical about this," she suggested. "Right now, you're an emotional, hormonal mess…"

"Gee, thanks," I said sardonically.

Mya cocked her head at me again. "Well, you are," she, so rudely, pointed out. "So, let's try to take all the emotion out of is. Can you do that?"

"I can try." At this point, I was willing to try to look at this from all angles.

"Now that you've slept with Callum, now that you've been married to him and have made a child together and experienced the horrible loss of that child…now that you know he's a complete, moronic idiot, but loves you, do you really believe you'll be okay walking away from him and watching him create a new life with someone else?" Her words were causing images I didn't want in my head. "Do you really want to be Callum's *ex-wife,* Chloe?"

The twitch in my chest was painful when I pictured everything Mya was saying. Our families were intertwined in a way that we'd never be free from each other. Even if it wasn't every single one, there would be times when we would run into each other during Christmas or Easter, family birthdays and milestones. I would even be expected to attend Callum's wedding.

His *real* wedding.

Every time there was a family function, my ex-husband would always be around and so would his ex-wife. I couldn't speak for Callum, but I knew every time I'd look at his children, I'd think about the one we never got to hold.

I would literally have to extract myself from Callum's life completely and that would include turning away from his parents, Timothy and Darlene. The thought made my heart ache something terrible. The Rosewoods were my second family…hell, they weren't even my second family; we were all one big family. It's the reason Callum was able to convince me to marry him due to the pregnancy. I hadn't wanted to ruin anything.

"I just want the hurt to go away, Mya," I whispered, tears gathering in the corner of my eyes.

"I get that, Chloe. I can't imagine what you're going through, but I do get what you're trying to say," she said, her voice strong and sympathetic. "But do you really believe walking away from Callum will make it go away?"

"I don't know," I admitted. "That's the problem. I just don't know what to do, Mya."

"Chloe, I think if you divorce Callum you'll only be trading one kind of hurt for another."

"I just don't know how to forgive how cruel he was. I know I sure as hell can't forget it," I mumbled.

Mya took a deep breath, and she folded her hands in her lap like a proper debutante. "Okay. I wasn't going to do this, but...tough love and all." I steeled myself for what she was about to say. She nodded towards me. "That scar on your face..."

I reached up and automatically touched it. "Yeah?"

"I remember the story you told me about how you got it," she stated. "That scar is a genuine accident. You and Callum were messing around and he accidently sliced your face open, right?" I nodded. "And in a fit of unchecked emotions, hurt, anger, pain, whatever...you went after the boy and cut his face wide open." I winced at her rather graphic, cold accounts of how Callum and I came to have matching scars on our faces. "He didn't deserve it, but because he understood how upset and emotional you were, he didn't tell on you, he didn't hold it against you, he didn't get you in trouble, he didn't do anything other than make sure you were *okay* even after you had just tried to gut him."

"My-"

She held her hand up to stop me. "At eight years old, Callum understood that you really didn't try to hurt him, that you were just emotional and upset. I would think that at as a grown woman, you'd be able to try to understand the same thing."

"Mya, that's not fair," I pointed out. She was comparing an incident that happened almost 20 years ago.

"Chloe, I'm not siding with Callum," she tried to explain again. "What he did was horrible. But he acted that way because he was pissed and confused. He doesn't think you're the type of woman who would trap a man, just like you don't think he's the type of boy who would physically hurt his 8-year-old best friend on purpose."

"I don't know what to think," I whispered quietly.

"Okay, well...let's forget thoughts for a second and focus on facts. Callum's said he was sorry for how he treated you. Either you forgive him, or you don't. There's no in between. He's told you he wants to remain married to you. Well, again, either you want to be married to him or you don't. There's no in between with that either. And, Chloe, either you love him, or you don't. Make some goddamn decisions, woman."

Before I could reply, the front door swung open and Callum walked in. I twisted my head to get a look at him and I watched as he gave Mya a small nod and headed towards the bedroom.

He looked stoic and cold.

I turned back to Mya when I felt her get up off the couch. Her eyes flickered towards the bedroom and back towards me as she said, "And you owe him an apology." She put her hand up to stop whatever I was about to say again. "What he did, he did because he was angry and confused. When you told him you wanted to try, but then told him you changed your mind to just wanting some bedroom action, you did that to purposely hurt him. You weren't confused. You were scared because you were about to cave, so you went on the offensive." And with that, she grabbed her purse and walked out of my apartment.

I fell back against the couch and closed my eyes. I knew Mya wasn't mad at me. She was just doing her tough love thing.

And she was right.

I could wallow in my emotional confusion all I wanted, but the truth of the matter was, the questions were black and white, and I just had to be brave enough to answer them.

And I knew the answers.

I knew them, but I didn't know how to not be mad at him. I didn't know how not to resent him.

I was just so goddamn angry.

And sad.

*God, how I was sad.*

But I knew-maybe not now-but I knew, later down the road I would regret being Callum's ex-wife. I would regret wiping out everything between us and resorting us to be a couple of people who used to know each other and spoke politely at family get-togethers.

I didn't want to see Callum with a new wife.

I got up off the couch and headed towards the bedroom. When I reached the doorway, my heart sank down all the way to my feet.

Callum was packing.

"Wh…what are you doing?" And then a thought occurred to me. "Are you…are you traveling for work?" It wasn't a stretch. Callum was a brilliant attorney. It was expected that he'd have to travel every now and again, even if it was just an overnight trip.

He didn't look over at me. "No. I'm getting some of my stuff together. It's been a few days, you seem to be doing fine physically. You don't really need me here anymore."

My blood felt like a huge tidal wave starting at the top of my head and rushing to the bottoms of my feet.

*He was leaving.*

"Call-"

He yanked open one of the drawers he had helped himself to as he cut me off, "If you could just not, Chloe, that'd be great."

I stepped into the room and stood by the bed as I watched him throw some socks into his suitcase that was lying on the bed. "Not what?"

Callum did stop then and looked down at me. "Say whatever fucked up shit you have planned. Right or wrong, I don't want to hear how you just want to use me for dick and the rings on your finger don't mean shit." His eyes glanced down at my hand and then back up to my face. "As a matter of fact, why are you even still wearing the damn things?"

This was it.

This is what Mya was referring to when she said I had to make a decision. Now, while I wasn't going to apologize to Callum for what I said-because I *was* still pissed-I was finally going to make a decision and hope it wasn't too late.

And I prayed it was the right decision.

"I don't want you to go, Callum," I braved.

He let out a humorless laugh. "Yeah, well, I don't want my wife to see me as convenient dick until someone better comes along."

I instantly went back to where I was trying to crawl out of. "Yeah, well, and I didn't want my husband talking about how he was going to fuck another woman on our wedding night!"

The suitcase was picked up and thrown across the room until it made contact and slid down the wall, leaving a dent in the drywall. "How many fucking times do I have to tell you I'm sorry before you fucking believe me?!" he roared.

Okay. So, maybe, he is already paying the price for how he treated me.

I did my best to shake off my anger and do what Mya advised. I wasn't delusional enough to think Callum and I would never argue again, but right now was deciding the rest of our lives; it wasn't the time to argue.

I stepped to him and placed my hand on his heaving chest. "Callum..."

He shook his head at me and slapped his hand over the one I had on his chest. "You're killing me, Cee. You're absolutely fucking killing me."

"I know I've been all over the place, but in my defense, so have my emotions." Callum closed his eyes in a defeated surrender. I knew he thought I was ending this. "I'm so mad at you, Cee. That hasn't changed," I said, wanting to be clear about that. "But I lied."

His eyes snapped open and his chocolate orbs searched my face. "You lied?" I nodded. "About what?"

I took a deep breath and went for broke. "I lied about wanting to use you to heal. I lied about not wanting to stay married to you. I lied about only wanting you for sex. I lied about it all because every time I think about how you treated me these past couple of months, my pride rears its ugly head, and it makes me hate myself for still wanting to be with you."

Callum reached out and pulled me into his arms. His arms were like steel bands around my body, and any tighter, he'll be suffocating the life out of me. "I love you so fucking much, Chloe. So fucking much, and you will never know how sorry I am for reacting the way I did and accusing you of the things I did. And you will never fucking know how much I hate myself that you still lived-live in this building."

I knew he was referring to the baby. I needed to think beyond myself and remember that he lost a child too. "I know, Callum," I whispered. "I know."

# CHAPTER 18

*Callum*

It's been three weeks since Chloe admitted that she wanted to try to make our marriage and friendship work and it's been a fucked up three weeks.

We both went back to work that Monday after her miscarriage, and so, that took up most of our daytime hours, but we texted throughout the day. However, it was mundane shit like plans for dinner or letting each other know if we were working late. Granted, I was the one who worked late most days, but I knew that was the kind of life I was signing up for when I decided to become a lawyer.

The fucked up part was when I got home from work-we were still living at her place-and we circled each other in movements, shrouded in politeness and civility.

I hated it.

I wanted my Chloe back.

I wanted the Chloe who called me on my shit and wasn't afraid to push me away when I was annoying her. The Chloe who didn't treat me as a goddamn guest in her home.

Our parents were constantly stopping by and, at first, I thought it was to check on how Chloe was doing, but I finally realized they were coming around to make sure we didn't kill each other. But one of the good things about our parents knowing the truth, we didn't have to pretend around them anymore.

Our siblings were still in the dark and we still hadn't told them the truth, but they didn't need to know. Siblings were different than parents. Chloe's brothers were more likely to kick my ass and convince her to divorce me, while my brother and sister would kick my ass, but beg Chloe to forgive me.

Mya and Andrew made constant appearances, too. I wasn't sure about the motive behind Mya's visits, but Andrew was stopping by to make sure I wasn't contemplating throwing myself out the bedroom window.

I walked through the door and I could hear the pipes running through the walls. I held up my arm and checked the time on my watch. It was already past six in the evening, and so, Chloe must have already been home for a while.

She had a routine, and it's been the same since I could remember. Even when we were in school, she'd get home, do her homework-or work, work as was the case now-eat dinner before six, take a shower and then read or watch T.V. until she was ready to go to sleep around nine. She wasn't a fanatic about her routine; it was just her routine.

I headed into the bedroom and started undressing, getting ready for my own shower. I had already eaten at the office and was just ready to unwind and finish off this work week. I had plans to work a little tomorrow, but I planned to work from home. Well, Chloe's home.

I had kicked off my shoes and removed my socks and jacket before going to work on my tie. I was pulling it off my neck when Chloe walked out of the bathroom wrapped in only the towel on her head and the towel wrapped around her body.

I managed not to groan, but my dick was crying in my pants. He was so pissed at me and I didn't blame him. I was doing my best to respect Chloe and give her space, and my dick wasn't appreciating the sentiment at all.

And he wasn't really appreciating my commitment to give Chloe space when she walked up to me-still in only a towel-and reached up to take hold of my tie, helping me remove it from my neck. She had no idea what she was doing to me, and if she did, then she must still be angry as fuck with me to torture me like this.

Her hands started unbuttoning my dress shirt, and I was about to beg for mercy when she looked up at me and said, "I took a long lunch today for a follow-up doctor's appointment."

My entire body stilled. I absolutely had no idea if her visit garnered good news or bad news. The worst scenario possible started playing around in my head and it felt like I was starting to drown. Whatever came out of her mouth, I prayed it wasn't bad. "And?"

As she finished with the last button, Chloe lowered her head until she was staring at my chest and running her hands inside my shirt to push it out and up over my shoulders. It fell in a quiet flutter to the floor. And then she ran her hands back over my shoulders and down my chest until she was caressing my abs.

My heart started racing and my breath became uncontrollable.

Chloe stepped closer until her towel encased tits were pressed up against my ribs. She looked up at me and almost brought me to my knees. "He said I'm doing well, and I'm cleared to…try again."

"Chloe, don't fuck with me," I growled. I didn't think my heart could take it.

My breath caught, and I was pretty certain I was on the verge of losing my mind when I stared in utter shock as Chloe reached for my belt while lowering onto her knees.

*Holy fucking shit.* Chloe was going to suck my dick.

*Willingly.*

But as much as I wanted her lips around my cock-and believe me, I wanted it very much-I was determined not to continue fucking this up. We were not going to go from uncomfortable roommates to sexual partners who still had issues.

I know she said she wanted to try, but I knew she was still feeling hurt over my behavior towards her, no matter how she was trying to get over it. So, there was no way I would let us use sex as a bandaid on an amputated leg.

I reached down to pull her to her feet. "Cee-"

And that was all she wrote folks.

Chloe already had her lips wrapped around the head of my dick and all good intentions and rational thought fled like they were being chased by the police.

Call me weak, but I let out a strangled groan and dug my hands into Chloe's hair, knocking off the towel that was sitting on top of her head, and let Chloe suck my dick.

She had one hand wrapped around the base of my cock, while the other hand was gripping the front of my right thigh. I probably should have been doing my best to work my pants off and get naked, but as far as I was concerned, all that could wait.

Chloe had her mouth wrapped around my dick, trying to swallow my length, and I was not going to do anything that might halt her determination. There was a good chance that if I so much as hinted to moving this to the bed or transitioning this to anything other than the blowjob she was giving me, she might stop and change her mind altogether.

Screw doing the right thing.

I tightened my hands in her wet hair. "Fuck, yeah, Cee," I groaned. "Suck my dick, baby." She moaned, and that small, seductive sound caused my hips to move. I started taking over and began fucking that luscious mouth of hers and she wasn't fighting me on it, either.

Chloe just kept working my cock with her mouth and tight, little fist as she made the most incredible sounds in the back of her throat.

And it felt like fucking Heaven.

I already knew Chloe could suck cock like a pro, but this time we weren't drunk. We weren't fighting. We weren't angry. We weren't forced. We weren't any of those things.

We were just being us. Me, Callum and her, Chloe.

Chloe was on her knees before me because she wanted to be; because she wanted to start over and make things better. She wanted my dick in her mouth for pleasure and to bring us closer together. Chloe wanted to try. And, while I expected talking as the form of communication that we'd be using to work our shit out, I'd take this kind of communication over what I had in mind, hands down.

She hadn't been down there, not ten fucking minutes, when I could already start to feel that sure-fire tingling starting to consume me. "Chloe, baby, I'm going to cum," I warned her. I knew she wasn't shy about swallowing my load, but new territory here…I didn't want to take a mile if she was only giving an inch.

Chloe held on like a champ and upped her tempo to make *sure* I was going to cum in her mouth. Her fingers of her free hand were digging into my thigh as she did her best to deep throat my fucking cock and as soon as I felt the tip of my dick hit the back of her throat, my shit shot out like a motherfucking cannon.

My fingers dug into her hair and I held her head firm as I jerked and spasmed inside her mouth. I could hear her gagging, but I was beyond common courtesies at this point. She wanted to suck my dick until I came, well, that's what she got.

As I closed my eyes to bask in the aftermath of my climax, I could hear Chloe's quiet purring as she licked my cock clean. When the shutters finally subsided, I looked down and Chloe was looking up at me with the most pleased look on her face.

I reached down and, grabbing her underneath her arms, I hauled her to her feet. I didn't want to ruin the moment, but I needed clear, precise direction right now. The whole mile and inch thing. "Why?"

She ran her hands up my chest and anchored them around my neck. She gifted me with those gorgeous blue orbs of hers and said, "If I take out everything except that first night together; the night of your graduation, it's everything I can do to keep from throwing myself at you, Callum. You're the best thing I've ever experienced naked."

*Fuck. Yeah.*

Chloe just admitted that I'm the best fuck she's ever had. If that didn't give me hope for a new beginning, then I didn't know what would.

I wrapped my arms around her body and held her close. I couldn't help my smirk. If you're a man, you'd totally understand. I leaned down and kissed her cheek until my lips touched her ear. "You like how I fuck you, Cee?"

I felt her shiver and her fingers started playing with the back of my neck. She stretched on her toes so she could reach my ear this time. "I *love* how you fuck me, Cee."

I didn't waste any time.

My feet took two steps back, and I was yanking the towel from her body and throwing her on the bed before she even knew what hit her.

In the three steps it took for me to reach the bed, my pants were already off, and we were both naked. I worked my knees between her legs and forced her legs to spread for me. The entire thing took maybe five seconds, but I was finally covering Chloe's body with mine.

Like I was always meant to be.

I was braced on my elbows, looking down at her as she opened her thighs wider, making room for me. "I love you, Chloe." I know she knew. But I didn't care. I planned on telling her every day for the rest of her life, so why not start now?

I watched as her eyes glossed over, but my girl didn't let me down. "I love you, too." Her breath hitched. "I've always loved you, Callum."

The pressure behind my eyes was real, but instead of giving into the sorrowful emotions threatening to take me under, I slid my cock into her pussy, and I knew I never wanted to leave it.

"Callum..." she moaned as she closed her eyes and threw her head back against the pillow.

I reached back and hooked her right leg over my arm, opening her up further so I could go deeper. I wanted to be so deep in this woman, she wouldn't know where we separated. "Like that, baby?"

Her head rocked from side to side. "God, yes," she breathed. "Just like that, Callum."

I pushed into her, and not in that frantic fucking kind of way. I pushed and pulled out of her like we had all the time in the world. I was so desperate for her, my first instinct was to fuck her like a paid prostitute, but just because the doctor gave her the okay, that didn't mean she wasn't still sore or whatever from her ordeal.

I didn't want to hurt her.

I wanted to make sure she was completely healed and able to take a good hard fucking later. So, I worked my cock in and out of her tight, hot pussy with a pace so steady, I was pretty sure I'd be officially insane by the time we were done.

"Callum, please..."

I kept rocking into her. "Please what, baby?"

Her hands latched onto my biceps and she squeezed. "Harder, Cee," she begged. And then she opened her eyes to look at me. "Fuck me harder, Callum."

"I don't want to hurt y-"

"Please," she begged again. "The doctor said I was fine. Please, Callum." Her fingers dug into my arms. "I promise to tell you if it hurts."

*Fuck.*

I leaned down and kissed the side of her face. "I got you, baby," I promised her. "You never have to beg me, Chloe. Whatever you want, whatever you need, it's yours." I started slamming into her warm sheath and it was all I could do to keep from cumming, even though I just came not ten minutes ago. Hell, I had wanted to high-five my dick when he got hard almost immediately after Chloe told me how she loves the way I fuck her.

"Like that, baby?" I asked. "Is that how you want to get fucked?"

Her nails broke the flesh of my arms. "God, yes!"

And, so, I fucked her. I fucked her hard and thorough. I slammed into her until she had given up two orgasms and I still wasn't done with her. I wanted her never to regret her decision to give me another chance.

I didn't cum until I had forced a third climax out of her, and she was screaming her apartment building down. I pumped everything I had into her unprotected body and I prayed she'd be pregnant by morning.

# CHAPTER 19

*Chloe*

I woke up and regretted stretching as soon as I did it. My body was so sore, but deliciously so.

Last night had been a perfect beginning to putting all this crap between me and Callum behind us. I mean, I knew sex wasn't going to solve everything, but it was a step in the right direction. I was able to be with Callum without thinking about the past or worrying about hurt feelings or what ifs. Mya's advice was spot on when she told me I needed to man up and make some concrete decisions.

I wasn't so delusional that I didn't think my emotions wouldn't make random appearances here and there, but I was confident I knew the difference between being emotional and being confused now. I wasn't confused about wanting Callum in my life and in what capacity. I wanted him as my husband. I've always wanted him as my husband. I wasn't going to give that up over something that time would heal, eventually.

Looking up at the ceiling, I could hear noises coming from the kitchen. My apartment wasn't very big, so privacy wasn't a real thing here, and you could hear just about everything throughout the place. I just prayed the walls were thick enough to muffle last night's acrobatics. If not…well, my neighbors just got to know me a little bit better last night.

But it was all worth it.

Callum was a fucking beast in bed and I didn't think I'd ever get enough of him. It wasn't just the size he was packing, either. It was everything. The way he knew just how to touch and where to kiss. The entire experience was soul consuming. Or, maybe, it was because it was Callum. He's the only man I've ever loved, so it could be that.

That's not to say I didn't care about the men I've been with, because I have. I cared for them deeply. But knowing that my heart had belonged to Callum since we were kids, well, that had always held me back from falling completely.

And, I guess I was right in that respect, because here we are, and after everything that Callum's confessed, it was hard not to believe we were meant to be.

I sat up and threw off the covers, deciding to be a big girl and face the morning after. When I stood up, I spotted Callum's dress shirt on the floor where we left it yesterday and I decided to do the total girl thing. I walked over, reached down, and put that puppy on.

The second I was enveloped by his scent, I realized what the big deal was. No wonder women wore their boyfriend's/husband's clothing, there was a sense of closeness in doing so. Now, never having done it before, I never saw what the significance was, but I do now. It was a way to be with Callum even when I couldn't be.

After throwing my ratted hair up in a bun, I brushed my teeth and splashed some water on my face. It's not like Callum hasn't seen me at my worst, but I was still feeling a bit girly about last night.

Making the best of my looks, I proceeded to paddle my happy ass to the kitchen, and the sight was one I'd seen a million times. Only this time, it was my husband making breakfast for me, and not my best friend. And the sight was a thousand times better.

"Hey," I said, greeting him as I headed towards the fridge for some juice.

"Hey, are y-"

I turned to face him when he stopped mid-sentence and I couldn't help the blush that coated my cheeks. Callum was looking at me as if he's never seen a naked woman before. "Are you okay?"

His eyes took me in, starting at my face and making their way down to my toes, and back up again. "That shirt has never looked that good on me," he breathed.

I smiled and did my best seductive sauntering towards him. "Is it because green looks good on me, or because you know I'm not wearing anything underneath?"

I could see his Adam Apple bob up and down. He kept his eyes on mine as he reached out, stuck his hand between my thighs, and then ran it upward until his fingers met my soft flesh.

The moan that escaped was real. Even though I was sore, his touch was enough to make me decide to soldier through the discomfort. And as if he could read my mind, he asked, "Are you sore, baby?"

Hell yeah, I was sore.

But not that sore.

I placed the juice bottle on the counter and ran my hands up his bare chest as he kept gliding his finger back and forth through my tender folds. "Not sore enough to ask you to stop," I answered. Callum had spent all night inside me and I found it still wasn't enough.

Callum removed his hand from between my thighs, grabbed me by my hips, and planted my ass on the counter. My legs opened of their own accord and Callum stepped right up in between them. He placed his hands on the tops of my thighs and leaned forward, kissing the column of my neck.

I dropped my head back to give him more access.

Shameless, I know.

His hand found its way back between my legs and Callum went back to rubbing my wet flesh. "You know, I'm not exactly sure how I'm supposed to function in life, knowing I can have you whenever I want."

I barely had a coherent thought. "What do you mean?"

"I mean, how am I going to be expected to go to work every day for hours on end after knowing what it's like to really be with you, Cee?"

The way he said 'what it's like to really be with you' had my heart thumping a heartbreaking tattoo. God, we were so stupid to have treated each other the way we have been. "I'm down to be broke and homeless if you just keep doing that with your fingers."

I could feel Callum's shoulders shake. His laugh had always been one of my most favorite things about him. "Jesus, Chloe, I'm trying to seduce you here," he said pointedly, all the while as he laughed.

I pulled my head up and dropped it on his shaking shoulders. "Is that what you're trying to do?"

He didn't answer. Instead, he slid his fingers from within my body, grabbed my thighs, and yanked my ass to the edge of the countertop. I closed my eyes against his shoulder as I heard him push down his pajama pants and free himself.

With my head rested on his shoulder and his head rested on mine, neither of us uttered a word as he slid into me. He was agonizingly slow about it, but it felt so good.

I wrapped my arms around Callum's neck and held firm as he slowly rocked into me. Everything felt different. We weren't frantically tearing at each other's clothes or coming together like wild animals.

Callum had his hands digging into my hips, his face next to mine, and I could feel his harsh breathing tickling my ear. Our silence made every thrust front and center to everything else around us. There was no dirty talk, or kissing, or playing to take away from the solitary feeling of Callum's movements. I felt every inch as he entered and receded from my body. I felt every ache and every connection.

I didn't know what we were doing, but here in the kitchen, on the countertop, half dressed, we were not fucking. We were not having sex. We were not making love.

I think we were saying sorry.

Suddenly, tears gathered at the corners of my eyes, and my arms tightened harder around him. I wanted to hold him. I wanted to hold on to this. Whatever this was.

"Callum..." I choked out.

And he knew.

He must have known, because suddenly, his fingers dug deeper into my hips and his movements became harder, deeper and more frantic. He was trying to tell me with his body what I refused to listen to in the form of his words.

Callum loved me.

He really, truly loved me, and this entire thing had been just one big fucked up mess. He didn't want to lose me anymore than I wanted to lose him. He didn't want to see me with a new husband anymore than I wanted to see him with a new wife.

I couldn't stop the sobs.

I couldn't stop how I needed to cry for the both of us.

"I love you, Chloe," he panted in my ear. "I love you, *so fucking much,* Cee."

"I know," I panted back.

The rest of it was done without another word spoken and the silence was so intense, I was sure my feelings would burst out of my body to disrupt it.

I'm not sure how long we stayed like that, but years later, I felt the pressure building in my core and I knew-I just knew-this would be the most intense thing I'd ever experience with this man. "Callum, I'm going to cum," I warned him.

"I know, baby," he whispered back. "I can already feel your body tightening around me. I can feel *you*."

And just like that, everything I was feeling exploded throughout my being, and I held onto him with every inch of body. *"Callum…"*

*"Goddamn it, Chloe."*

*"Oh, God, yes…"*

Callum's body seized and shuttered as he emptied himself inside me. He kept pushing inside me until he had nothing left to give, and even then, he didn't remove himself until a few minutes had passed and he started softening.

Our heavy breathing was the only thing that could be heard in the room, and I wasn't quite ready to break the silence and put an end to our little bubble.

I wasn't given a choice, though, when Callum pulled back to look at me. His hands came up, and he smoothed my flyaway strands of hair back from my face. I smiled, and he leaned in to kiss me. The kiss was sweet, tender and full of promises I never thought he'd make to me.

The kiss was a promise of a future together.

"That was…" I didn't really know how to describe it without sounding like an overly emotional female.

"Yeah, it sure was," he said, smirking. But then his expression turned serious. "I love you, Chloe. I love you like you'll never know. I want you to know that. I *need* you to know that. And I need you to know that I will never fucking hurt you ever again."

"Cal-"

"No," he said, stopping me from interrupting. "I know in the years to come I'm going to piss you off something fierce. I know I'm going to irritate the fuck out of you. I know I'm going to get on your nerves and I'm pretty sure there'll be times where I'll come home to my clothes being thrown out of the window." I laughed. I couldn't help it. "But it'll be because I love to annoy you, and never again, because I hurt you."

I untangled my arms from his neck and held his face in my hands. "Callum, I've known you all my life. You can be a real dick sometimes." He threw his head back and laughed. I just stared at his carefree reaction and it warmed my heart. When his gaze returned to mine, I continued, "So, I'm pretty sure there's going to be some hurt somewhere in our future, but I know it'll be nothing we can't get past."

He smirked as he let me go and grabbed his pants to pull them up, covering that appendage I've come to love so much. "Fair enough, Cee," I conceded. "But no running, okay?"

I knew what he was getting at. We can fight, we can cry, we can rage, argue, sulk, pout...all of those crazed emotions. But we couldn't run away from our relationship. We couldn't run from us.

I was so down with that.

"No running," I agreed.

Callum kissed my forehead and then stepped back. "Okay, go get cleaned up." He slapped the side of my knee and grabbed my waist, helping me off the countertop. "I'll sanitize the counter and finish breakfast," he said, laughing.

I cringed. "Yeah, that probably wasn't the best decision."

Callum really laughed then. "Chloe, I've spent countless hours with my face buried in your pussy. I couldn't care less if there are...uh, signs of you on the kitchen counter."

*Oh. My. God.*

I slapped his shoulder. "Are you out of your mind? That is so gross!"

Callum stepped away from the counter and turned back to finishing fixing breakfast. "Please," he snorted. "If you think that's gross, wait until you see how shit's going to go down when you're on your period."

I could feel my eyes bugging out. "You're going to stay the hell away from me while I'm on my period," I informed him. "That's how shit's going to go down during that time of the month."

He pointed the whisker at me. "See, that's one of the times where I might come home to find my clothes being thrown out the window." His chocolate peepers scanned up and down my body. "Because, baby, there's no way I'm going to go one night without fucking you, much less five. Or however many days that thing lasts."

I headed off towards the bathroom to clean up, but we were not done with this conversation. "You are not touching me when my period comes," I hollered behind me.

"Then I'll just be sure to keep you knocked up so that motherfucker never comes," he said, and I could hear the bastard's laughter even after I shut the bedroom door on his craziness.

I'm not going to lie, though. Once I was on the other side of the door, I couldn't stop the smile that spread across my face.

This is what I wanted. What I've always wanted with Callum. I loved him so much and I was beginning to believe that this was finally the real us.

## CHAPTER 20

*Callum*

Yesterday had been perfect.

After breakfast, we had showered and spent the day watching the Bourne Identity franchise movies. It was one of the things I loved about Chloe; she liked all types of movies, so I never got stuck on chick flick duty.

Now, we were at her parents with everyone in attendance. Well, everyone that was family. Me and Mya hadn't had our come to Jesus moment yet and I think Andrew was still annoyed at me. Every time I've called him, he's asked if I got my shit together yet.

Then hangs up depending on my answer.

"What are you doing?"

I glanced up from my phone. "Sending a text to Andrew, letting him know I finally got my head out of my ass," I answered, making Chloe roll her eyes.

"We're going to have to have a friendervention and all sit down together and kiss and make up," she said, giving me a pointed look.

I knew she was referring to me and Mya more so than her and Andrew. Hell, I think even Andrew and Mya got along. I'm pretty sure I was the only asshole out of this foursome. "I agree." Fuck, I'd agree to anything Chloe wanted at this point.

"I'm glad to see you two in a…better place," Mrs. Slater announced as she walked up to me and Chloe.

Yesterday, when Chloe had told her father we were working things out, he had called for a mandatory barbeque, and only imminent death was excuse enough to miss it. I'm not sure if they had wanted to actually see for themselves that Chloe and I were no longer contemplating murdering each other, or if we were just due for a family get-together.

So, now, we were all convened in the Slaters' backyard like we've been countless times before. I leaned in and kissed her on her cheek. "We're perfect, Mrs. Slater," I assured her.

I could see the stress visibly leave her body. "Oh, thank God," she breathed. "It was all I could do to talk Anthony out of killing you every day, Callum." She placed a hand on her chest. "And it didn't help one bit when your father was giving Anthony tips on how to hide your body."

Chloe grimaced, while I laughed.

I knew Mrs. Slater was, on some level, serious about my dad and Mr. Slater wanting to murder me, but I didn't blame them. I knew their stance on how a man is supposed to love the woman he marries, and I failed big time. The only reason I knew I was half-ass forgiven was that Stephen and Anthony Jr. weren't over here beating me to a bloody pulp.

"It would be no less than I deserve, Mrs. Slater," I said, smiling at the beautiful woman. Mrs. Slater was a knockout.

"Hey, Mom, Dad's calling for you," Stephen announced walking up to our group.

Mrs. Slater shook her head. "Of course, he is. It's a wonder how the man functions without me around," she teased before heading off to look for her husband. And I had to feel for Mr. Slater. I wondered how he functioned without her too, because it was bothersome enough when Chloe was out of my line of sight, I couldn't even imagine how Mr. Slater felt without Mrs. Slater around.

Stephen threw me a head nod. "How you treating my sister, Cal? We haven't spoken much since your wedding. We all kind of figured you were still honeymooning it even if you guys did stay home."

I tried not to wince. Even if Chloe and I hadn't gone through what we did, I still didn't want her brothers avoiding her because they believed we've been doing nothing but fucking all this time. "You're going to have to ask her," I answered.

Stephen looked over at his sister. "How goes it, Sis? Do I have to kick his ass?"

Chloe laughed. "We're fine, Stevie," she assured him. "But it's nice to know I have you and A.J. on standby in case he forgets to put his dirty socks in the hamper."

I watched as Stephen wrapped his sister up in a huge hug that is distinctively a sibling move. "I'm glad, Chloe. I always knew you guys would end up together."

She stepped back to look up at him. "Did you now?"

He smiled at her. "Yep. I even bet A.J. when we were in high school. You should have seen how devastated he was when he had to pay up at your reception."

"What d'you guys bet?" I asked.

"Twenty bucks," he answered, happily. "In high school, twenty bucks was high stakes, my friend."

"I wonder if Tim and Darlene had a bet," Chloe mumbled.

Before I could comment, my phone chimed. I looked down to see that

Andrew texted me back.

*U better not b lying asshole*

*I'm not!*

*You made it right?*

*Yes!*

*If ur lying, I'm going 2 kill u…just so u know*

*Fine. Now quit being a little bitch*

*If I'm a bitch, ur a bitch*

I laughed. Andrew was good for me.
Chloe glanced my way. "Everything good?"
I smiled at her. "Everything's perfect."
"Oh, God," Stephen groaned. "You guys are sickening. Really."
I smirked at my brother-in-law. "I'll remember that when you get married."
Stephen rolled his eyes. "Even if I do get married, it won't be with a woman I've known since we were in diapers. There's no way we'll be as disgusting at you two."
"Callum!" I looked over to see my dad waving his hand in a 'come here' gesture.
When we had arrived, we had been busy being wrapped up in hugs and catching up with Chloe's brothers and my sister and brother. Stephen hadn't lied when he said they had all been holding off, letting us enjoy our so-called honeymoon. Except for a few random texts, here and there, our siblings had pretty much stayed away.
So, when we arrived, we were immediately bombarded with well wishes and inquiries on married life and all that jazz. Even though Chloe and I were the youngest out of the hoard, none of our siblings were married. Not one of them was even in a serious relationship right now. They all blamed their careers, but I think sometimes when you come from a big family, you forget you can be lonely for a different kind of love.
I wondered how long it would be before my father pulled me aside, and I have to admit, he lasted longer than I thought he would. I kissed Chloe on the side of her head, and leaving her with her brother, said, "I'll be right back, baby. I'm going to go see what my dad wants." She just nodded her head, and already forgetting about me, followed Stephen to go join the rest of the clan.
My dad wasted no time.

The second I was standing before him, he kicked off the interrogation portion of the afternoon. "How's Chloe doing?"

It didn't surprise me that his first question was to see how Chloe was doing. I was the baby of the family, but my wellbeing was a distant second to Chloe's. "She's doing fine, Dad," I answered. "She had a doctor's appointment on Friday where her doctor cleared her physically."

Mark Rosewood let out a deep gruff. "What about mentally and emotionally, Callum? How is she doing there?"

I knew my dad was still disappointed in me, and it stung. It stung badly. "I'm working on both of those, Dad," I promised. "But she's doing fine."

He grunted as he looked over at her with her standing with the rest of the family. "You sure about that, son?"

I let out a deep breath. "Dad, we're talking and we're working it out. It's not going to turn into perfection overnight, but we're trying."

My father looked back at me, and the determination in those eyes of his that matched mine, caused my breath to hitch. "Callum, I'm going to tell you something, and I will only tell it to you this one time," he started out.

I swallowed and just nodded at him to let him know I was listening. I knew this was going to be him with the gloves off. My mother wasn't around to soften his edges.

"That girl is the best thing that has ever or will ever happen to you," he stated, and I felt like a fool that he felt he needed to tell me something I already knew. "She is the best parts of her mother and father, and The Slaters are the best people around."

The more he spoke, the more I felt like a heel, because I knew all this already.

"Anthony and Natalie have forgiven you in a way I don't think I'd ever be able to if someone did to Darlene what you did to Chloe." Is it possible for your heart to bleed, but stay alive? "And the fact that Chloe's forgiven you…well, you better learn how to live on your goddamn knees, son. She deserves it."

"I know, Da-"

"Shut up, Callum," he barked.

*Fuck.*

He stepped into my personal space, and as if he wasn't the man who changed my dirty diapers, he stared at me in a way he's never challenged before. "If I *ever* hear that you've mistreated that girl again, I will not protect you from your brother, sister or the Slater brothers," he stated, seriously. "I will not protect you from Anthony or Natalie. And I, sure as fuck, won't protect you from Chloe."

"Dad, I-"

"Callum, I need you to shut up and hear me," he said, interrupting me again. "If you ever treat Chloe so horribly again, I will do everything I can to help her move on to a man who will treat her like she deserves," he continued, shocking the fuck out of me. "Do you understand me?"

I love my father.

I was fortunate enough to be raised by parents who knew their roles and embraced those roles the best way they knew how. Gina Rosewood was the perfect balance of nurturing and stern, while Mark Rosewood was the perfect balance of protector and role model.

But, right now, in this moment where he's telling me he would support Chloe with someone else, all respect and common sense fled.

Even as I knew I deserved this dressing down, and even as I was very aware of my treatment of Chloe, no one was going to take her from me. I had already expressed to this before to both our parents when I had confessed what I'd done, but I guess my father needed another reminder.

I took a step towards him until we were practically nose to nose. "I will always regret how I treated Chloe. It's something that will haunt me until the day I die, but I meant what I said, Dad. No matter what life holds in store for us in the future, I will never let Chloe leave me. *Never.* And I will fuck up anyone who ever tries to take her from me or stands in my way of keeping her." I was pissed. "And that includes you, her father and her goddamn brothers. Chloe is fucking mine. Do you hear me? *She's. Fucking. Mine!*"

I hadn't realized I was yelling until I felt Chloe latch onto my arm. "Callum!"

I didn't turn away from my father. He had to see how serious I was. Chloe was my goddamn *life!*

If was a few tense seconds before my dad smiled and Mr. Slater let out a hoop and holler somewhere off in the distance.

*I'd been played.*

I let out a deep breath and shook my head.

I'd been played by our fathers *and* they got me in trouble with Chloe.

Five…four…three…

"What the hell is your problem? Why are you yelling at your dad?" she barked.

My dad clapped me on my shoulder as he walked away laughing, leaving me to explain myself to Chloe.

*The asshole.*

"He was giving me shit, and-"

Her brows shot up. "That's no excuse to speak to your father lik-"

I grabbed her arm and whipped her around until she was standing directly in front of me. I looked down at her stunning face and that goddamn scar and it was all I could do to stay upright. "He threatened that if I ever treated you like shit again, he was going to help find you a new man to live happily ever after with, Cee."

Her face lost all righteousness. "Oh."

"Yeah, 'oh'," I parroted.

She began chewing on the inside of her cheek. "Sooooooooo…"

"You're mine, Chloe," I pulled her into my arms. "You're mine and not one person here is more important to me than you are, baby."

## CHAPTER 21

*Chloe*

"I know I can be dense sometimes, but how I managed to miss that fucking rock on your finger is beyond me," Benedict said in a way of greeting as he planted his ass on the chair across from my desk.

I held my hand up and watched the diamonds glitter. It's been a couple of weeks since Callum and I made up and it's been the best kind of couple of weeks.

"Well, remember that wedding I told you I went to last month?"

He bent his right leg over his left at the ankle. "Yeah, your best friend's," he said, remembering.

"Well, I neglected to mention I was the bride at his wedding," I said sheepishly.

Benedict barked out a laugh. "That's a hell of an omit."

I felt bad. I considered Benedict a friend, not as good a friend as Mya, but a good friend, nonetheless. "I'm still kind of getting used to the idea," I explained lamely.

He cocked his head at me. "So, what? Was it like an arranged marriage or something?"

This time I laughed. "No," I clarified. "It's nothing like that." Since I couldn't tell him the truth, I tried to go with something semi-believable. "I love Callum very much, it's just strange to refer to him as my husband when I've been referring to him as my best friend for 26 years."

He nodded. "I get it, but I don't," he quipped. "But as long as you're happy, Chloe, I'm thrilled for you."

I smiled because I knew Benedict was genuine with his congratulations. "Thank you, Benedict."

"So, when do you get to meet this mystery man?"

"Soon, I promise. Maybe the next work bashing session," I answered.

"Sweet!" he exclaimed like a teenager before getting up and walking out of my office.

I'm glad he didn't ask too many questions, because I knew I didn't have answers for most of them. Mine and Callum's start was not a happy one, and I wanted to gloss over that as people were going to begin to find out about us.

The phone on my desk rang, and I answered when I saw the screen identifying Mya. "Why are you calling me on my work phone?"

"Ugh," was her first reply, her second being, "because I feel like crud soup and I didn't bother putting any real effort into working my phone. I told it to call you and it picked this number all on its own."

I let out a soft laugh. "You sick?"

"I wish," she replied, all dramatic-like. "If I was sick, I'd down some Nyquil and call it a day." Nyquil was awesome for that. "I started my period and I feel like a…period monster."

This time my laugh wasn't so soft. "Is there such a creature?"

"Yep," she said, popping her 'p'. "I swear, Chloe, the only good thing about growing old will be when this torture comes to an end," she went on with her dramatics.

"Too bad we have to experience menopause for that to come to be," I reminded her coldly. "That's going to be a whole other bitch to deal with."

"Why are you trying to squash my silver lining?" she whined.

"I'm just trying to keep your feet planted in the real world, Mya," I answered, reminding her of how great a friend I was.

"Just wait until you start yours, I'm going to dance on your bloody tampons and cackle in delight," she threatened…so very vividly.

"That's just distur-"

My period.

Holy. Crap.

*My period.*

"Chloe?" I could hear Mya's voice coming through the phone, but it was faint noise behind the realization that my period was late. "Chloe, are you there?"

"Uh," I had to clear my throat. "I…I'm here."

She must have sensed something was wrong, because she asked, "What's wrong?"

My hands were tangled in the phone cord in a white-knuckle grip. "Mya…"

"Jesus, Chloe," she breathed out, sounding a bit panicky. "What's going on? You're scaring me."

"Mya…I…" I let out a swoosh of air. "I think…I haven't had my period since the miscarriage. It's been…I should have by now…"

All of Mya's bemoaning vanished in an instant. "Okay," she said, sounding like a general taking charge. "Okay. So, it's been what a couple of week-"

"Five, Mya," I corrected her. "It's been five weeks."

"Okay, but…you just recently suffered a miscarriage," she whispered.

"Can't that interfere with your normal cycle or something? Maybe your body is still healing, and it skips or…fuck, Chloe…I don't know."

As inopportune as it was, I laughed. God love Mya for trying to logically calm me down, but it was clear we had no clue what the effects of a miscarriage were. "I'm going to call my doctor an-"

"Yeah, you do that," she urged. "You go do that right now. As a matter of fact-"

She hung up on me.

I laughed as I realized Mya hung up on me.

I knew she was panicked and hung up so I could call the doctor, but it still brought a smile to my face to know I wasn't experiencing this alone.

I set down the receiver and grabbed my cell to call my doctor. It was the phone that contained all my contacts. I had fallen into that debilitating habit of not memorizing phone numbers anymore.

His office answered on the third ring. "Good Morning, you've reached Iris Women's Health. This is Kayla speaking. How may I help you?"

"Hi, Kayla. This is Chloe Slater…uhm, Rosewood. Uhm, Chloe Slater Rosewood…"

"Oh, Chloe," she greeted. "It's good to hear from you. How are you doing?"

"I'm doing well," I lied. "I was wondering if Dr. Melcos had a quick second to answer a question for me. Or even Imelda." Imelda was Dr. Troy Melcos' nurse practitioner, and the lady knew her shit.

"Dr. Melcos is with a patient right now, but I know Imelda is in between appointments. Let me put you on hold, Chloe."

My relief was palpable. "Thank you, so much, Kayla."

"No problem. Just give me a sec," she replied before putting me on hold. I knew it wasn't easy to get through to your doctor when you didn't have an appointment, so being able to get through to Imelda was akin to a goddamn miracle.

What was I going to do if I was pregnant?

What was I going to do if I wasn't?

Callum and I hadn't spoken about birth control or our plans for future children…I mean, I still wanted children, but this just seemed so soon. Had my body even healed enough to be able to maintain a healthy, successful pregnancy?

The thought was terrifying.

The phone clicked into action before I could send myself into a frenzy of nerves and what ifs. "Chloe?"

I sighed. "Good Morning, Imelda."

I could hear the smile in her voice. "Good Morning, Chloe. Kayla said you had some questions for Dr. Melcos?"

"Uhm, yeah," I had to clear my throat again. Panic was setting in. "I…well, you know…I had that…"

She took pity on me. "I'm very aware of your medical history of late, Chloe."

My throat was dry, and it was hard to swallow. "Yeah…well, the thing is…" *Just fucking spit it out already!* "It's been about five weeks and I haven't started my period yet. Is that normal?"

Imelda went into full-on medical mode. "Chloe, every woman's body is different. When a woman experiences the kind of changes and/or trauma that comes with conceiving and disengaging the healing process varies from woman to woman as a result of lots of factors."

*Disengaging?*

What a clinic way to refer to losing your baby. But I supposed it was her way of trying to keep things calm for fear of me breaking down in tears over the phone.

"Well, what's the general healing time and wait? You know, just your average textbook."

"It depends on how long you bled afterwards, for starters," she explained. "Whether you're having unprotected sex or-" My breath hitched. I hadn't meant for it to, but it just did. "Chloe, are you having unprotected sex?"

"Uhm, maybe?"

"You're asking me?" she questioned, chuckling.

I let out a deep sigh. "Fine. You caught me."

Imelda continued to chuckle. "A lot of unprotected sex?"

"Uhm…well, how much do you consider a lot?" I felt like I was in the principal's office.

"Chloe, as a woman in this medical field, I have to tell you, even one time is a lot," she scolded.

I knew she wasn't going to be able to help me if I wasn't completely honest with her. "I started having sex again about two weeks ago. And, uhm, well, we don't use anything." That last sentence was uttered in a whispered tone.

"It seems unlikely considering everything your body's been through, Chloe. However, why don't you come in this afternoon for a quick urine test? We can draw some blood, as well, but those results won't be back for a day or two. But since the urine tests are pretty accurate, the blood test results will just be confirming what we'll already know."

I gulped. "Wha…what time?"

"Can you come in around one o'clock or so?"

I nodded before I realized she couldn't see me. "Yes, I can be there…"

"Okay, then we'll see you later today, Chloe," she confirmed.

"Thank you, Imelda," I replied.

"You're welcome, Chloe," she said right before hanging up.

The second the line cut off, I dialed Mya. "What?"

I laughed. God, I loved this woman. "I just made an appointment at one to take a test."

"What did your doctor say?"

"He was busy, so I spoke with his nurse practitioner and she wasn't much help," I answered. "She gave me the standard 'everyone's body is different' explanation and so she suggested I come in for a urine and blood test today."

"Do you want me to go with you?"

Once upon a time I would have said yes. But now that Callum and I were trying to get right with each other, it felt wrong having Mya go with me while Callum didn't even know. I knew he might be upset about finding out I went alone, but I was pretty sure he'd be hurt if he found out I asked Mya to go with me instead of him. "No, that's okay. I'll be fine," I assured her.

"Are you going to tell Callum?" She wasn't one to tiptoe around the hard topics.

"No. I don't want to freak him out or get his hopes up," I admitted. "We never really *talked* about the baby and losing it and all that. We've expressed how hurt we were, but I've never told him the details of how devastated I was-am. And all he's said was that he was in mourning, too."

"Chloe," she sighed. I knew I was about to get lectured again. "I know you guys are treading lightly, and I know you guys have come a long way with talking and working things out, but you guys have got to mourn your loss together to be able to heal and move on from it." I hate when she makes sense. "Chloe, you cannot be afraid to talk about children with your husband."

Of course, I knew Mya was right. If Callum and I were going to remain married and work towards a future, that future was going to include children at one point. Like Callum had so ruthlessly pointed out on our wedding night, he's always wanted a few kids. Three was his magic number. I knew this. I've always known this.

I think we were both just too afraid to bring it up for fear of blame being thrown around. I didn't blame Callum for the loss of the baby once. I blamed him for believing he didn't want us. I never once thought he was the cause of all this, though.

Whatever our fears, Mya was still right. "I know, Mya. It's just…uncomfortable," I mumbled lamely.

"You want to know what's uncomfortable? Having to tell your husband you're pregnant again when you've just started to move forward together," she harrumphed.

"Fine," I conceded. "I promise to talk to him this evening no matter what the tests results show this afternoon."

"Chloe, babe, you know this is the right thing to do," she insisted. "I know it sucks, but you and Callum have to exorcise everything about those dark weeks."

"I know, Mya. I know." There wasn't much more I could do other than watch the hands of the clock tick down, so I said, "Look, I need to go and do some speed working so I can take a long lunch or go home early and have a meltdown, depending on what happens at the doctor's. So, I'm going to go, but I promise to call you later."

"Okay, babe," she replied. "I love you and call me if you need anything."

"I will," I promised, then hung up.

Despite what I told Mya, it took me another 15 minutes before I was able to get my head back in the work game and put a dent in my day, and the next thing I knew, it was past noon.

## CHAPTER 22

*Callum*

I was doing my best not to lose my shit, but it was hard.

The weird thing about texting is that people say you shouldn't read too much into a text. It's a text. Like email or a letter, you miss the person's expressions and tone of voice. But the thing is, you can get a feeling from a text.

And I was getting feelings all afternoon from Chloe's texts

All kinds of feelings. And not the good kind.

They weren't out of pocket or anything, just really short and…short.

I even called her after lunch, and she seemed very preoccupied and…short.

Andrew said I was overreacting when I had called him earlier, but I knew this thing with me and Chloe was still fragile. Even though we've come a long way, we were still treading lightly. We haven't even really talked about losing the baby and how we're each dealing with that because the wounds were still very fresh.

So, her one-word texts were making me antsy.

I walked into her apartment and I immediately wondered when I would find the balls to approach moving to my place. It's not that I didn't like her apartment, I just felt that as long as we still had two separate residences, we weren't really all in like we claimed. My place was just so much bigger that it made sense that we'd live there. One day we were going to have children, and we were going to need all the extra space.

"Chloe?" I hollered as my eyes took in the empty kitchen and living room. I waited a few seconds, and when she didn't answer, I headed back towards the bedroom. My heart sank when I spotted her sitting on the bed, still fully dressed in her work clothes, wringing her hands and staring at her lap.

Something was terribly wrong.

For Chloe to be so deep in her thoughts that she didn't say anything when

I called out for her, something had to be wrong.

"Chloe?" She didn't look up, and she didn't stop wringing her hands. Her eyes stayed transfixed on her lap and it was enough to cause me some panic.

I dropped my briefcase, rushed towards her and dropped to my knees in front of her. "Baby?"

Her head lifted slightly, and when her eyes met mine, I was so thankful I was already on my knees. I would have surely dropped from the fear and sorrow written all over her face.

She didn't utter a word and my first thought was that something must have happened to our parents or siblings. "Chloe, baby, what's wrong?" I cradled her face in my hands. "You're scaring me, Cee."

Her eyes watered, and the biggest crocodile tear I've ever seen cascaded down her right cheek. "Callum…"

Still on my knees, I inched closer to her. "What, baby? Tell me what's wrong," I asked her again.

"Cal…I'm…I'm…" Another crocodile tear fell down her left cheek, matching the sorrow of the first.

"Jesus Fucking Christ, Chloe," I begged. "I'm going crazy here."

Her hands came up and wiped the tears from her face. I watched as she took a deep breath and did her best to collect herself. After what seemed like 20 billion agonizing seconds, she whispered, "I'm…I'm pregnant, Callum."

"You're pregnant?" I'm pretty sure I heard her correctly, but this was not a thing to misunderstand.

"I…uh, I was talking to Mya on the phone this morning and she sort of went off on the miseries of being on your period and…" She took a deep breath. "Well, midway through her rant, it occurred to me that I haven't had a period since…I, uh, stopped bleeding."

She was killing me.

*Absolutely. Killing. Me.*

She sounded terrified to be having this conversation with me. I placed a hand on each of her knees. "It's okay, Cee. Go on," I said, hoping like hell my words would calm her some.

"I wasn't sure how it worked," she went on. "You know, after going through something like that, so I called my doctor, and they told me every woman was different and…"

I leaned in a little closer. "And…" Her eyes searched mine, and I knew she was looking for signs of anger or resentment. I fucking hated that she was uncomfortable talking to me; especially about being pregnant with our child.

"Imelda, the nurse practitioner, suggested I go in and take a urine test and get some blood drawn," she continued to explain. "So, I did. I…uhm, I took a long lunch and went."

The first words that wanted to come out of my mouth were to ask her why didn't she call me, but I knew why. She still didn't trust me with her feelings. She still didn't trust me to keep her safe, and that stung like a goddamn motherfucker.

While, Chloe had every right to be wary and protect herself first, it still hurt like a bitch.

"Is that where you were when I called you today?" She nodded, confirming my assumption. "Okay," I said as smoothly as I could. "What happened? I mean, I know what happened…but, I mean, what did they say? How accurate are the urine test results?"

"Imelda said the blood test results are more of a confirmation of the urine test results. I'm…Imelda said it's pretty much a guarantee that I'm pregnant again, Callum."

I knew how I felt about the news. I wanted to jump up and down and fist pump the air. Chloe was pregnant again, and we were going to have a baby and do it right this time around. I wanted to laugh, and cheer, and call our parents.

But instead, I asked, "Why are you crying, Cee?"

Her breath hitched, and the tears started flowing again. "I…I'm scared, Callum," she whispered, breaking my fucking heart.

My hands left her knees and went back to cradling her face. "Scare of what, Chloe?"

"I'm scared something might happen to this baby, too," she confessed. "What if…"

I knew the promise I was going to make was a hollow one, but I did it anyway. "Nothing is going to happen to our baby, Cee. I promise."

"You can't know that, Callum," she argued.

"Yes, I can," I replied, unreasonably. "We didn't…we didn't work things out and forgive each other to…" Christ, I couldn't even say it.

"And what about…" Her eyes darted around the room and I felt my heart crack in two. Chloe was scared about losing the baby, but she was nervous about something else. I waited patiently until her eyes returned to mine. And when they did, she said the most painful thing she's ever said to me, because I was the cause of her next words. "I feel like I'm trapping you all over again," she whispered and the pain I felt was very real. I let go of her face, and dropping my head into her lap, I wrapped my arms around her hips.

Chloe was afraid to have children with me.

*My wife was afraid to have fucking children with me.*

I did enough damage to her in those two months of me being an asshole to make her believe that I didn't want kids with her. She thinks I'll see them as a burden or an anchor to a wife I didn't choose.

I could feel the pressure behind my eyes, and I wanted to cry like a fucking baby. I wanted to cry for the loss of my first child, the loss of my childhood best friend, the loss of trust from my wife…the loss of a lot of fucking things.

I couldn't believe I ruined so much love between me and Chloe with my bullshit.

But I ruined more than that. I ruined the trust we used to have between us. I ruined the connection that had made us best friends.

I ruined her faith in me.

Chloe's hands started running back and forth over my shoulder blades. "Callum?"

I tightened my arms around her hips and just stayed how I was for a couple of minutes. There was so much I wanted to say. There was so much I wanted to take back and apologize for. There was just so much I needed to say to her.

I needed to tell her how much I regret treating her the way I did. I needed to tell her how much it hurt to lose our baby. I needed to tell her how I knew this was all my fault and I needed her to forgive me.

But nothing I say is going to matter if she didn't believe me.

I finally lifted my head and told her the truth. It didn't matter if she believed me or not, because she deserved to hear it. "I know I've said this already, but I'll say it every day for the rest of our lives, if I need to, in order for you to believe me. I love you, Chloe. I've loved you since before I knew what love was. And the second I knew what it meant to have children, and that I wanted, at least three of them, I knew I wanted them with you." She started crying again, but she didn't interrupt. "You were always going to be the mother of my children, Chloe. Just like you were always going to be my wife."

"Callum…"

"*Please,* Cee," I implored. "I need to say this. I need you to hear it. And I pray you believe me when I'm done." She nodded for me to go on. "I…I know it's my fault you lost the baby and I can't tell you how brutal my regret is."

Her eyes widened. "Callum, no," she whispered, horrified. "How can you say that?" Her tears really started falling this time. "You weren't the…the one who…you're not the one who was stupidly moving a desk…" Chloe's voice started to hitch, and she was full on sobbing now. "It's m…mmm…my fault we lost the ba…baby." She dropped her face in her hands and cried. "It's all my fault, Cee. I lost our baby."

I stood up, sat on the bed, and dragged her across my lap until I had her cradled and plastered to my body. I rocked her, and at the same time, wished for the ground to swallow me up. Every word felt like she was carving up my insides. I can't believe I did this to her.

I didn't deserve anything from Chloe.

"Cee, it's not your fault," I said, praying she'd believe me. "It's mine. If I hadn't reacted the way I did, if I hadn't been such a fucking asshole, this never would have happened." She was bawling into my chest so hard, I wasn't even sure she could hear me. "If I hadn't been so blinded by stupidity, I would have moved you into my place the second you told me you were pregnant. You would have been living with me and you would never have been here to help Mrs. Burke with that goddamn desk."

She tried to burrow herself farther into my chest. "C...Callum..."

"Baby, this is all *my* fault and I pray you can forgive me someday," I admitted and begged.

Chloe cried for what felt like hours on my lap. And I let her. As long as she was allowing me to hold her, I'd let her cry until the sun came up tomorrow.

I'm not sure how long we stayed like that, but she finally stopped the sobbing and her cries had turned into heartbreaking whimpers. She snuggled deeper into my arms before finally speaking. "W...we both sh...should have...have taken better care of the baby. I...I think we...we both made some mistakes. Mistakes we're both always going to regret."

Thank God I was sitting down.

Chloe wasn't blaming me. Well, not entirely.

And she was going to forgive me.

I tightened my hold on her and kissed the top of her head. "I swear to God, Cee, I will spend every day of the rest of my life taking care of you and our children. I will never put pride before what is best for you and our kids. I'm not going to lie and say I'll never fly off the handle or that we'll never fight, but I swear that's all they will ever be...*just arguments*. I'll never be cruel and vindictive and make you pay for something that...well, I'll never make you pay for anything."

"God, what a mess," she uttered softy.

I situated her until she was straddling me, and I could look into her eyes. We *weren't* a mess. "Chloe, we *were* a mess. That goes without saying. But we're not anymore. We're...a bit rattled and unsure, but we're not a mess."

She tried to lighten the mood. "Oh, I'm a mess," she laughed out, sadly. "I'm definitely a mess."

I smiled. "I'll admit, I've seen you look better..." She laughed a real laugh this time, and that's what I was going for. "But you're still so fucking beautiful, Cee."

Chloe blushed, and that was saying something since her face was all splotchy and tear stained. Her fingers came up to caress my jaw. "Not as beautiful as you are, Callum," she whispered. "You really are the most magnificent man I've ever seen."

*Thank fuck.*

It wasn't that I cared overly much about my looks, but I wanted to be the only man for Chloe. I wanted to be the only man that made her run, crawl, beg and surrender. And with how badly I fucked things up, I wasn't above using my looks to keep her hooked.

I tightened my arms around her hips. "I love you, Chloe. I love you and I love the baby we had and the baby we're going to have. I want a million kids with you. And, if God is willing, I want them all to look like you."

She huffed. "You want short, fat kids?"

My eyes narrowed. "No," I bit out. "I want beautiful, healthy, perfect looking kids, Cee. And that's what I see when I look at you. I see nothing but what is perfect in my life."

Her face softened. "I love you, Cee."

I smiled. "We're going to have a baby, Chloe," I announced as if she didn't know. "We're going to have a baby and, this time, we're going to celebrate the shit out of this." And then something occurred to me. "I'll even give you a real wedding, if you want, Cee."

Chloe wrapped her arms around my neck. "I don't need another wedding, Callum. I just need this right here. This, with you."

## CHAPTER 23

*Chloe*

We kept my pregnancy a secret until my fears had subsided, which took about three months. Callum was patient and understanding about it, but I knew he was desperate to shout it to the world. Or, at least, tell our families about the baby.

But he didn't.

The only people who knew were Mya and Andrew because, since Mya had already known because of the phone call, it was only right that Andrew knew, as well. I didn't mind, though. The news was too big to keep it just between the two of us.

It wasn't that I didn't want our families to know. I just didn't want to break everyone's heart in the event something went wrong. I had gotten pregnant almost immediately after a traumatic miscarriage, there was no guarantee that my body wouldn't reject this pregnancy as it was still trying to heal.

We hadn't been total secretive hermits this entire time, though. During these past few months, we managed to move me out of my apartment and into Callum's condo and now his place no longer looked like a bachelor pad. I got rid of most of my furniture but held on to all my sentimental purchases. The condo looked like a perfect blend of me and Callum.

The nursery was all Callum, though. And as much as I had wanted to take part in its creation, it had been something that Callum had wanted to do alone. I knew his need was born out of how he still blamed himself for the miscarriage, so I relented. Partly because I still felt pangs of guilt and hurt when something would happen, and I thought back on how I didn't get the chance to experience these things with our first baby. I was healing by taking baby steps, while Callum was healing take big leaps.

Plus, if Callum was set on having three kids, I knew I could be a part of the nursery decorating then. I was just so…nervous about everything.

I felt Callum's arms wrap around me from behind over my slight bump. "How are you feeling?"

Today we were going to tell our families about the baby, and it was a big step. You wouldn't think it'd be that big a deal…I mean, it was our families. They loved us, and this was going to be a good time; great news. But…my trepidation was real.

I wrapped my arms over Callum's. "I'm nervous," I admitted.

He dropped his chin on top of my head. "I know you are," he replied. "So am I, if I'm being honest."

"Are we being stupid?" I asked, because I felt like we kind of were. I was four months pregnant, and according to the doctor, the baby and I were both healthy and everything looked good. Callum and I were in a good place and…well, maybe that's my problem. Maybe everything was just looking too good to be true.

I could feel Callum kiss the top of my head. "We're relatively stupid most days, Cee," he teased. "I'm sure today will be just fine."

"You have a good point," I joked back.

Callum turned me around in his arms so I was facing him instead of the bathroom mirror. His smile was sweet, encouraging and real. "Look, Cee, there's a lot of residual stupidity still lingering about, but we're not stupid in being together."

"I just feel like some days I'm so bogged down by my emotions that I don't even know my own mind," I shared with him.

"Awe, Chloe," he whispered. "I think you'd feel that way even without all the bullshit we went through. It's called pregnancy, babe."

I couldn't stop the little laugh that escaped. "You're a dick," I pointed out, needlessly.

"True," he agreed. "However, I'm your dick, so that makes me a special kind of dick."

I shook my head. "You make no sense, at all."

Callum stepped back, turned me back around, and slapped my ass. "Hurry up and finish getting ready," he instructed. "I told my parents we'd be there at around two."

He walked back into the bedroom when I called out, "I wouldn't mind being a little late," I said with enough sass to let him know what I was thinking.

I could hear his laugh from the bedroom and then his voice come through loud and clear. "I have no problem spreading your legs open and burying my face in your pussy, Cee. But know that if that's the reason we're late, that's the reason I'm giving our parents."

*The bastard.*

He would, too.

"Fine," I hollered back.

"You'll thank me when you're not blushing from head to toe in front of the parentals," he laughed.

Ever since we found out I was pregnant, the sex has been...delicate. Callum spent a lot of time with foreplay-not that I was complaining-than he did with actual sex. And when we did have sex, it was slow, sensual and careful.

We had spoken with my doctor about it, and even though he assured us that it was perfectly safe to have aggressive sex, he was more concerned with my mental state than anything physical. Dr. Melcos had explained that stress was my biggest enemy and if we were so worried about sex being detrimental to the baby, then it might very well be. He recommended doing what we felt was comfortable for us as a couple. He made it clear that he didn't want me under any undue stress whatsoever.

So, that left a lot of oral sex, and while it was fantastic, I missed the frantic desire; the dark need. Sometimes I could see it in Callum's eyes. I could see how he just wanted to bend me over and drive into me. And the yearning seemed to increase with each change to my body.

One thing I was absolutely certain about was that my pregnancy turned Callum the hell on, and that knowledge did so much for my peace of mind. I already had body conscience issues, so knowing my breasts were going to get bigger and that I was actually going to be gaining so much more weight had really been messing with my mind in the beginning. But Callum really seemed to love my body the way it was, and at one point, he had said the bigger I got, the more of me there was to love. He also said that if it bothered me that much, he'd volunteer to be my exercise program.

The pervert.

I finished throwing my hair up and applying my makeup and then headed into the bedroom to grab my shoes. Callum was stuffing his wallet in his back pocket, looking every bit the male he was.

I walked over to the closet, but couldn't help but say, "I hope you still want me after this baby is born and my body goes all to hell."

The fucker snorted.

"Chloe, the second the doctor gives you the all clear, I'm dropping that baby off with our parents for a week and I'm going to spend every second of that week with you under me," he smirked.

I grabbed my sandals and turned to look at him. He was standing with his hands on his hips, looking at me. "Is that so?"

He arched a brow. "Yeah, Cee, that's so."

"And what happens if I decide to breastfeed?" I asked, teasingly. "How's that week with our parents going to work then?"

Callum smiled. "Okay, Mrs. Hardball, I'll give you an hour each morning to pump your milk out and Andrew and Mya can take turns delivering it to our parents."

My laugh bent me over. He was so ridiculous. When I was able to catch my breath again, I asked, "Are you seriously saying you would turn Mya and

Andrew into a breast milk delivery service?"

Callum walked towards me. "Hell, yeah, I would."

Once he was standing in front of me, he grabbed me by my shoulders, and sat me on the bed. I watched as he knelt down and put my sandals on for me.

My heart skipped a beat.

He spoke as he connected the straps. "I love and want you beyond how you see yourself, Cee. I love your heart, soul and mind. Your sexy as fuck body is just a bonus." He grabbed my other foot and worked on securing the other sandal. "As for wanting you, while I lust after your body, it's your soft moans that I'm always eager to hear. It's your whimpers that make me lose my mind. It's how your pussy gets soaking wet every time I tell you how I'm going to fuck you like a dirty slut."

I felt my skin tingle, and I itched to rub my thighs together to relieve the pressure his words were causing. "Callum…"

He finished with my shoe and looked up at me. He must have seen my desire written all over my face, because he said, "I've jerked my dick off to images of you since I was fucking 12 years old, Chloe." My heart raced, and my body warmed. "And after that first night together, it was all I could do not to break down your door and just fuck you senseless, knowing how it finally felt to be inside you." His hands clasped my ankles, and slowly worked their way up my legs, over my knees and inside my thighs.

I shamelessly opened my legs wider.

Callum's hands didn't stop until his thumbs snuck under the sides of my panties and he was rubbing my pussy lips, ignoring my clit, driving me crazy. My hands grabbed his shoulders and there was no coyness here. My hands anchored to his shoulders to keep in place. I didn't want him to stop whatever it is he was about to do. "Callum, please…"

He took mercy on me and let his right thumb finally make contact. "That right there, Cee," he said, applying more pressure to my clit. "When you beg…when you moan for me…that's what I live for." I was about to beg some more when his instructions sent chills down my spine. "Lay back for me, baby."

I did.

I dropped back onto the bed as if someone had pushed me. That's how eager I was for Callum to put his mouth on me.

I closed my eyes and waited in anticipation as Callum worked to lift my skirt over my stomach and pull down my panties. It felt like an eternity before he finally placed his hands on the inside of my thighs, pushing them apart, and opening my center for his use.

"See, Chloe, your pussy is the prettiest thing I've ever seen. When it's open like it is now, when it's glistening because you love it when I tell you how dirty I'm going to make you…that beats the size two you think you need to be." Callum started his ministrations with one long, slow, torturous stroke across my pussy from the opening of my core to my hard, ready clit.

I moaned. It felt so goddamn good. "Mmmm, Callum…"

He added two fingers into his oral play and soon he was finger fucking me while his tongue played with applied pressure to my clit.

I spread my legs wider.

I wanted more.

I wanted Callum to fuck me unconscious, even though I knew he wouldn't.

I missed his rough fucking. I missed the bruises and bite marks.

He pulled his mouth off my body. "I'm going to always want you, Chloe," he stated right before he went a step further.

To my surprise-and pleasure-Callum removed one of his fingers from my pussy and inserted it into my ass. I let out a deep breath, but I didn't tell him to stop. He's made no secret of the fact that this was something he wanted. Something we were going to do in the future. I needed to get used to this kind of play, especially since it was something I wanted also. I've never engaged in anal play, but I wanted to with Callum.

I wanted complete inhibition with my husband.

He put his tongue back on my clit, and the next thing I knew, he was double penetrating me with his fingers as his tongue pushed me to the edge.

My hands dug into his scalp. *"Callum…"*

He removed his mouth from my pussy only long enough to ask, "You like that, baby?"

I wasn't going to lie. "Yes," came the sluttiest moan I've ever heard come out of my mouth.

"Good," he said, encouraging me to lift my hips for some more. "I'm going to make you love it when I finally get my cock into that tight ass of yours."

That's all it took.

It could have been the hormones, his filthy words or his skilled tongue and hands, but whatever the trigger, sparks started flying throughout my body and I could feel myself clamp down on his invasions. "Callum…" I mewled as my hands tightened in his hair.

"That's it, baby," he cooed. "Soak my fucking face."

And I did.

I gave myself over to every tremor, shake and shutter. After a few moments, my body sank into the bed and I just laid there, my breathing the only thing resonating in my ears. My silent ecstasy was interrupted by the sounds of running water, and a few minutes later, I felt Callum's body weighing down the bed beside me.

"I can't be kissing my mother's and your mother's cheek with that mouth, or shaking our fathers' hands with those fingers," he said, chuckling.

I cringed. "Oh, God." The man had a point, though.

Callum laughed. "Come on, Cee. Get cleaned up and let's get going," he said, helping me sit up. "Just think, the soon we get this over with, the sooner we can get back here so we can continue this." He winked at me and pushed up off the bed.

I gave him my best stink-eye as I headed towards my dresser drawers for a new pair of panties. "You are pure evil, I hope you know," I grumbled.

Callum's smile lit up his face. "Yeah, but I wouldn't be if you didn't love it so much."

"Ugh," I, neither confirmed, nor denied and went to clean myself up..

# CHAPTER 24

*Callum*

We arrived at my parents a little late, but I wasn't complaining. Had this not been important, I would have stayed buried in Chloe's pussy for the rest of the afternoon.

It was déjà vu again with everyone in my parents' backyard, only this time, Andrew and Mya were here, too. Even though they already knew, we thought we'd recruit them in a little deception and asked that they act surprised when we told our families.

We weren't out to hurt anyone's feelings, and we knew that if our families found out that Mya and Andrew knew about Chloe's pregnancy before they did, they'd be hurt. Sure, they would accept our reasons at face value, but I knew they'd be hurt; our siblings more so than our parents. It was common knowledge that siblings were the ones you kept secrets with, not the parents.

I hadn't necessarily agreed with Chloe on keeping her pregnancy a secret, but I understood where she was coming from. She was still scared despite being passed the first trimester and the doctor's assurances that everything was fine.

"Hey, if it isn't the prettiest girl around and the sorry sap she's chained to for life," my brother, Tim called out.

Chloe wasted no time hurrying towards him and letting him wrap his arms around her. "Hey, Timothy." She leaned up and kissed his cheek. "How's my favorite Rosewood male? Well, except for Mark, of course."

Tim let out a hearty laugh. "I'm doing great, Chloe. And, uh, now that you mention it, you're the prettiest girl around, save for our mothers."

I chuckled as I clapped my brother on his shoulder. "Best to clarify that, Tim."

He rolled his eyes in relief. "Don't I know it," he sighed.

Chloe laughed. "You guys really are terrible. I don't know how Darlene ever grew up to be a beautiful, normal functioning human being."

"Right?" My sister's incredulousness was exaggerated just like her spunky personality. "It's a wonder how I made it through my childhood without therapy. These two assholes are *horrible*."

I hugged my sister and then stepped aside so Chloe could get at her next. "Watch it, Sis. We can still cause untold damage to you if we put our minds to it," I threatened.

Darlene threw her hands up in surrender. "Relax, Cal. There's no need to threaten me with a good time."

"Oh, my God!" Mya exclaimed as she came rushing towards us. "It's about time you showed up." She placed her hands on her hips and let out a deep sigh. "I was one more 'women are meant to be taken care of' comment away from murdering Andrew, Chloe," she announced. "I was not looking forward to having to explain to the police how I was forced ruin this lovely barbeque because Andrew Cambridge was a certified moron."

Before any one of us could respond, the certified moron was already standing next to her ready to make his case. "How the hell am I a moron because I think women are meant to be taken care of?"

Mya rounded on him and left the rest of us to watch in awed fascination. "Because you're making it sound like we belong in the kitchen, barefoot and pregnant," she thundered.

Andrew bore down on her. "I did not *say* that!"

I saw my father coming up behind Andrew and clasp a hand on his shoulder. "Just tell her she's right, son. Tell her she's right and walk away real nice and slow," he advised.

Me and Timothy started laughing, while Chloe gave me the stink-eye, Darlene crossed her arms over her chest and Mya growled.

Honest to goodness growled.

Our two friends drew a crowd, because the next thing I knew, A.J. and Stephen were standing next to my father. "What's going on?" Stephen asked.

Timothy snorted. "Andrew forgot the cardinal rule that all women are right all the time," he quipped.

I watched as A.J. and Stephen, both, visible winced. "Not a smart thing to forget," A.J. chimed in.

"Oh, for the love of God," Chloe snipped, rolling her eyes. "You men are so goddamn ridiculous."

"Yes, we are, dear," my father agreed, all the while smiling at her.

"Well, hell, since we're all here," I started. "Mom! Mr. Slater! Mrs. Slater! Can you guys please come over here?" I didn't have to yell too loud. They were already on their way over to see what the gathering was all about. It wasn't too farfetched to assume one of us was about to pummel the other. We were six siblings with four of us being men. There was never a shortage of scrapes, bruises and black eyes.

As they all gathered, Chloe snaked her way over towards me, until she wrapped her arms around my waist, and I had my left arm anchored over her shoulders.

It's crazy to me how we've held each other like this so many times before, at a million previous family barbeques, but this time it meant so much more.

I looked down and saw she was looking up at me. My eyes darted to the scar on her cheek and I realized, in this moment, that it was my favorite thing about her. And that was saying something when I felt uncontrollably addicted to her sweet pussy.

"Have you ever thought about covering up that scar?" It sounded like a casual question, but it wasn't.

Her answer was going to mean everything to me.

Chloe squeezed me tighter. "Never," she whispered, and the conviction in her voice was all I needed to hear.

I gathered her up in my arms and our hug was the kind that was reserved for goodbyes. Or second chance hellos. "I love you," I whispered in her ear.

"Okay, okay, okay," A.J. blathered. "We get it. You're in love. You guys have the perfect love everyone dreams of."

Everyone around us chuckled, and I released Chloe, but not entirely. I still made sure she was anchored to my side. "Fuck you, Anthony."

"Okay," Mrs. Slater said, "You kids knock it off, now."

My mother chuckled alongside Mrs. Slater. "What were you wanting to tell us, Callum?" She asked, getting right to the point.

I looked down at Chloe and she gave me a small nod and a smile. I took my time giving everyone I loved my attention, and when my eyes returned to my fathers, I smiled and announced, "Chloe's pregnant!" The gasps, laughter, hoots and hollering were thundering, just like I knew they'd be.

Chloe was pulled out of my arms by her mother and it was hugs all around after that. Everyone was congratulating us, and the reception was perfect. Our mothers were a mess, but that was to be expected, since they knew about the miscarriage. But everyone else reacted as expected.

My father pulled me aside as everyone started taking turns on molesting Chloe's stomach. "How are you doing with all this, Callum?"

I knew he was asking because of the miscarriage and mine and Chloe's rocky start and not because he wasn't thrilled or had faith in me. "I'm good, Dad," I answered honestly. "I know you guys are still a little concerned, but Chloe and I are doing really well. This...Dad, this...her, it's everything."

He gave me one of those manly hugs where he patted the shit out of my back. "I'm glad, son. That's all we ever wanted for you two."

I hugged him back. "I know, Dad. We both know."

My sister drew me out of our bonding moment. "Are you guys going to find out what it is, or be surprised?"

Chloe's eyes darted to mine before she looked back at Darlene. "We're going to be surprised," she announced. "We talked about it and...well, we consider ourselves blessed no matter what we have."

"Well, of course, it's a blessing no matter the sex," my mother jumped in.

"I think waiting is going to make this adventure so much more exciting!"

Mrs. Slater cleared her throat, and I knew what that meant. She was going to get feisty. "How ironic, our first grandchild given to us by our youngest children."

The grumbles could be heard all around the world.

"Goddamn it, Callum," Timothy groaned. "See what you guys did?"

"Yeah," Stephen joined in. "I'm going to have to spend the next nine months dodging my momma's matchmaking."

"Stephen Rosewood, don't make me take you over my knee," my mother threatened.

"Awe, Mom," he whined.

Chloe, bless her heart, jumped in to save Tim. "It's closer to five months, not nine."

"Oh, my God!" Mya exclaimed, happily. Even though she already knew about the pregnancy, she was still so over the moon about the news. "We're going to have a baby in five months!" Her eyes started misting over and I assumed it was because she could finally share her excitement.

"I can't believe I'm going to be an uncle," Andrew announced.

"Uh, you do know that this kid is going to have three other uncles, right," A.J. broke to him. "Me, Tim and Stephen are standing right here, dude."

Andrew waved his statement away. "Please…it's a given fact that Callum spends more time with me than he does you freaks," he countered. "So, by default, the baby is going to spend more time with me. Therefore, making me his favorite."

Mya's hands went back on her hips. "Wrong again, Andrew," she snarked. "Everyone knows the baby spends its first few months with its mother, bonding and being nurtured. And since I'm Chloe's best friend, that means the baby is going to be spending all its time with me first."

"Woman, I will battle you to the death if you dare taint that baby," Andrew growled.

I started laughing.

We all started laughing at the ridiculous pair.

It was sweet, but ridiculous all the same.

I threw my hands up in a calming manner. "Relax, folks. Everyone will have plenty of quality time with the baby when the time comes," I assured them.

"You say that now," Darlene huffed.

I looked at my sister. "The second the doctor clears Chloe after her six-week checkup, you best believe I'm dropping this baby off on one of your guys' doorstep."

"Callum!" Chloe cried, her face turning beet red.

"*Callum Rosewood,*" my mother admonished.

The men all chuckled, while the women all grimaced.

"Okay, okay," Mr. Slater said, hushing everyone. "Let's get this celebration started."

Everyone started making their way back to the patio where the barbeque was set up, leaving Chloe and me with some privacy. When everyone was far enough away, I looked down at Chloe. "How are you feeling? Are you okay? Still nervous? Anxious?"

She shrugged a shoulder. "I think I might be anxious until I can finally hold our healthy, happy baby in my arms." I nodded, because I knew how she felt. I felt it, too, to some degree. "But I'm not nervous about everyone knowing now. I'm…I'm actually happy to be able to talk to our moms about the experience of being pregnant. I'm going to enjoy watching Tim, Darlene, A.J. and Stephen buy things for the baby and share in our excitement."

I stepped around until I was standing directly in front of Chloe. I took her face in my hands and ran my thumbs back and forth across her jaw. "Cee, you're going to be fine. You're going to be fine and you're going to deliver me a healthy, happy, perfect baby," I insisted, hoping to finally get through her fears. "And after you do that, you're going to give me another healthy, happy, perfect baby." She laughed. "And after that, you're going to give another one."

She was laughing and crying. But she was crying happy tears. "You're so silly, Cee."

"Not this time, Cee," I replied. "Because, this time, I'm being so serious, baby. You're going to make me the most beautiful babies."

Her face softened but, then, became serious. "But…let's just say, what if I can't," she whispered, hauntingly.

I didn't care.

I mean, I cared if she couldn't, but I didn't care if she couldn't. All that matter to me was Chloe, first and foremost. I was going to love our children with my whole heart, but I loved Chloe with my whole heart, soul, mind and body.

"Then we adopt," I informed her. "Then we adopt as many kids as you want." She smiled so sweetly. "We adopt and do what we were meant to do if being biological parents aren't in the cards."

Chloe threw her arms around my neck and clung to me as I lifted her tiny body off the ground. "I love you, Callum," she cried in my ear. "I love you so much and it's going to be me and you."

"You're damn right it's me and you, Cee," I confirmed. "Me and you against everything else and every-fucking-body else. You and me, Cee. You and me."

I sat her down, and when she looked up at me, her face shone with happiness and real joy. "You know we're going to ruin this kid's life with all the things we don't know, right?"

I threw my head back and laughed. Of course, I knew that. I smiled down at her. "That's the reward in having two other kids, Chloe. We'll learn from our mistakes with the first and the second, guaranteeing that the third one has a fighting chance at life."

Chloe smiled back. "Maybe we should aim for four kids," she teased. "The fourth is, for sure, bound to come out mentally stable, don't you think?"

I looked down at the love of my life and said, "Four sounds perfect."

# EPILOGUE

*Chloe - Ten Years Later*

I didn't want to open my eyes.

I knew I'd overslept, and all I could picture was a kitchen exploding in cereal and milk, and one, two or all three of my children tangled in the blame game.

Callum and I had stopped at three kids, taking our chances that the third one would turn out relatively normal. If not…well, all children turn 18 years old eventually, and out into the world they go.

I kept my eyes closed but strained my ears to see if I could hear any yelling. Or crying.

Timothy Stephen Rosewood was nine. Anthony Mark Rosewood was seven. And Caylum Darlene Rosewood was five. Darlene and her husband, Robert, beat us with the daughter race and they named their little girl Gina. Stephen and his wife, Celine, had also kicked our ass in the daughter race, and they had swooped up the name Natalie.

So, by the time Caylum came to be, our mothers' names were already taken and so Callum begged me to let him name her after his sister. And him, of course.

I loved her name, but I never let him know it. There'd be no living with him then.

I heard nothing but silence and prayed my children were being model citizens and eating breakfast like decent humans are supposed to; with a bowl and a spoon.

But I wasn't one of those delusional parents. I knew my children were evil.

My eyes closed, I suddenly felt fingertips playing on my thigh over the bedsheet. I groaned. "Go away." Mother of the Year? Probably not, but I knew they wouldn't take it to heart. My kids were used to my need to sleep in.

Usually Callum took control on the weekends and let me sleep in, but he had said something last night about having to get up early to go help his parents with something or other.

"If I go away, how am I going to be able to bring you pleasure that only my tongue can bring?"

My eyes popped open and saw Callum was naked. "Did you forget the Timothy Rule?"

Callum chuckled.

When Timothy was two, he completely underestimated his ability to wake up on his own in the middle of the night and work a doorknob. The Timothy Rule was born the next morning and we've done what most parents across the country do; we sneak in sex when the kids aren't around. And if we can't hold off until we unload them on someone, we. Lock. The. Bedroom. Door.

Callum climbed into bed next to me and my body immediately started to hum. "I'll never forget the Timothy Rule, Cee. But I just came back from dropping the kids off with my father, begging him to do me a solid as one husband to another."

I laughed. "You did not!"

"The fuck I didn't," he countered.

We were going to have uninterrupted sex for the first time in months and I didn't know what the hell to do with myself. "Okay, if we're going to do this, I have to get up, go pee and brush my teeth," I announced, putting an end to the romance.

Callum let out a huffed laugh, "You know I don't care about your morning breath, but you have a point about getting up to pee. I'm not into…uh, that kind of sex play."

Even though I laid out my immediate plans, I didn't move from where I was laying. Callum was already kissing his way down my stomach and placing kisses along my hipbone. "Christ, you're so good at that, Cee."

I felt his lips curve against my skin. "Good at what? Loving you?" My heart melted at his simple questions.

Ten years, and three kids later, Callum was still holding true to his promise that he was going to worship me for the rest of his life. Sure, we had our fair share of arguments, but they were just like he said they would be…*just arguments*.

"You're actually pretty perfect at doing that, Cee," I admitted.

Callum nipped at my skin with his teeth. "You're damn right," he bragged.

"How much time do we have?" I asked as I felt him pull my panties off my hips.

"All fucking day, baby," he rasped out, causing me to moan.

I closed my eyes. "That sounds like just enough time."

"Chloe, all the time in the world will still never be enough time with you," he whispered.

And he was right.

A million years with Callum would never be enough.

The End.

# PLAYLIST

What Does It Take – Honeymoon Suite
Love Me Harder – Ariana Grande
This Woman's Work – Kate Bush
Fallin' – Alicia Keys
Angel – Aerosmith
Back For Good – Take That
Beautiful Soul – Jesse McCartney
Breathe – Michelle Branch
Broken – Seether
Call It Love – Poco
Darlin' I – Vanessa Williams
Girl Can't Help It – Journey
Hanging By A Moment – Lifehouse
I Can't Tell You Why – Eagles
I Shall Believe – Sheryl Crow
Life After You – Daughtry
Miracles – Jefferson Starship
Piano In The Dark – Brenda Russell
Rooms On Fire – Stevie Nicks
Say Goodbye – Jordan Knight

# ABOUT THE AUTHOR

M.E. Clayton works full-time and writes as a hobby. She is an avid reader and, last year, she decided to trade in some of those reading hours to try her hand at writing her first book. With much self-doubt, but more positive feedback and encouragement from her friends and family, the Seven Deadly Sins series was born and a hobby she is now very passionate about. When she's not working, writing or reading, she's being pampered by the best husband in the world, having heart to hearts with her son, giving her daughter life advice or spending time with her grandchildren If you care to learn more, you can read about her by visiting the following:

Smashwords Interview at:
 https://www.smashwords.com/interview/MonClayton
Bookbub author's page at:
 https://www.bookbub.com/profile/m-e-clayton
Follow my Goodread's author page:
 https://www.goodreads.com/MEClayton

# CONTACT ME

I really appreciate you reading my book and I would love to hear from you! Now, unfortunately, because I do have a full-time job, and a family I love spending time with, at this time, I'm afraid it would be very hard for me to maintain a multitude of social media sites. However, for the sites I do participate in, here are my social media coordinates:

Favorite my Smashwords author page:
 https://www.smashwords.com/interview/MonClayton
Like my Facebook author page:
 https://facebook.com/claytonbooks
Follow my Bookbub's author page:
 https://www.bookbub.com/profile/m-e-clayton
Follow my Goodread's author page:
 https://www.goodreads.com/MEClayton
Visit my Website at:
 https://meclayton2016.wixsite.com/mysite

# OTHER BOOKS

Please visit your favorite book retailer to discover other books by M.E. Clayton:

**The Seven Deadly Sins Series** *(In Order)*
Catching Avery
Chasing Quinn
Claiming Isabela
Conquering Kam
Capturing Happiness

**Stand Alone**
Unintentional
In Enemy Territory
Purgatory, Inc.
Facing the Enemy

Printed in Great Britain
by Amazon